13 Frights

13 Frights

Robert Freese

Stonegarden.net Publishing
http://www.stonegarden.net

Reading from a different angle.
California, USA

StoneGarden.net Publishing
3851 Cottonwood Dr.
Danville, CA   94506

First StoneGarden.net Publishing paperback printing:
October 2012

First StoneGarden.net Publishing electronic printing:
October 2012

Visit StoneGarden.net Publishing on the web at
http://www.stonegarden.net.

Cover art and design by Peter Joseph Swanson

The Frights

This effort is dedicated with
much love to Frances.

RWF

Deadlines

Rebekah's hands were cramping, burning, but she was afraid to stop, afraid to lose any more time, even a couple seconds, to rub them.

Her head hurt horribly. A dull aching thud banged behind her eyes and in her temples. Beads of sweat ran off her brow, stinging her eyes, but she refused to break her pace to wipe them dry.

The constant tapping on the keyboard filled the tiny room. It was adrenaline mixed with fear and caffeine that kept her fingers moving.

The clock on the gray block wall showed two forty.

There was no way it could already be two forty, her mind screamed.

Jabbing at the keyboard, Rebekah lost her train of thought. Reading the words on the screen she realized they made no sense.

Deleting the lines she shot a quick look up at the clock. It was two forty-two.

Two minutes wasted!

Concentrate! There is no time for mistakes, she reminded herself, no time to delete entire lines. There is no time to waste.

Trying to get back on track she re-read the last line of dialogue. Her mind kept straying to the ever-ticking clock. The words, all the words, were a jumbled mess.

None of it made sense. Nothing in the world made sense right now.

The only thoughts in her head were of Malcolm, of what they were possibly doing to him at that very moment. Today she had quickly realized how an insignificant seeming moment could change your life, a mere second. Lives were conceived in a moment, as well as taken, lost.

The screen stared unblinking at her in the gray room. Actually, her mind unconsciously straying from the words, it was more like a jail cell than a room. She was surrounded by four concrete block walls, all painted gray. There was the desk with the computer on it and the clock looming on the wall opposite the desk.

The clock on the wall.

Suddenly, at exactly two forty-five, the single door offering escape from the cell was kicked open.

"Pages," Joshua demanded gruffly.

Rebekah printed the four new pages of script she had completed and handed them to the big man.

"This is it?" he asked, looking over the four sheets.

"I'm doing the best I can," she blurted out. She had to stop herself from breaking into tears.

"Well, darling, your best better get a hell of a lot better, and fast, if you don't want hubby to suddenly kick his addiction to breathing." He put a paper cup full of black coffee on the desk next to the keyboard. "Drink it," he said, looking at his wristwatch. "An hour and fifteen minutes left."

A tear finally worked its way free and ran down her cheek.

"Darling, look, you know how this game is played. It's a minute per page. Each page of script equals a minute of movie time. For a full-length feature, Mr. Warwick needs at least ninety pages. You're only halfway through." He looked at the last page of the script.

"You've got fifty-one pages so far. That's not even an hour of movie time." He looked at his watch again. "Now you only have an hour and thirteen minutes left to finish up the last thirty-nine pages. That's..." he figured it up in his head.

"Jesus, darling, you're gonna have to write better than a page every two minutes to meet the deadline, and all we're doing here is wasting time."

Rebekah was getting frantic. Panic was squeezing her heart. This was madness. So much time had been wasted in that first hour, when she tried to tell herself it was all just a joke to scare her. Then she was forced into believing the severity of the situation, forced to believe with each of her husband's screams.

"Please, just let me talk to Mr. Warwick. I just need a break, a little more time. I know I can…"

Joshua cut her off.

"The only thing you can do for Mr. Warwick is finish his goddamn screenplay by four o'clock sharp."

"If I could just talk to him," she pleaded.

Joshua shook his head disgustedly.

"More incentive," he mumbled under his breath. Retrieving his cell phone he punched in a number.

"No," Rebekah cried. The tears were pouring freely now. "You don't have to do that."

"Yeah," Joshua said into the little phone. "Let's have another one."

Through the concrete wall Rebekah heard her husband's agonized wail.

A short man in thick glasses and slicked back hair rushed into the cell. Grinning, he handed Joshua a wad of blood-soaked paper towel.

"He's running out of these, darling." Joshua dropped the contents of the paper towel onto the desk like he had the others.

It was another one of Malcolm's fingers.

"Stop wasting time," Joshua grumbled and moved toward the door. Before leaving he stopped and turned back to her.

"And quit cheating the goddamn margins. If you keep on cheating, Mr. Warwick will be forced to tack on ten more pages to the script."

The cell door slammed behind him.

Hysteria was trying to get a firm hold on Rebekah. Swallowing hard, she forced herself to gain control of her breathing and stop crying. Hysteria was not going to help either her or Malcolm in this situation.

How could the world spin so wildly out of control because of just one phone call? It was one of those monumental moments, a second that changed a life.

She found her place and continued writing.

At three o'clock the cell door swung open. It seemed like only a few seconds had passed since Joshua left and now the man was back.

"Pages," he demanded.

Rebekah printed the new pages, left them in the printer for Joshua to fetch himself.

"Not bad, six pages. Mr. Warwick has some concerns regarding a number of loose ends the storyline is dragging out. He wants them all tied up by the end. And punch up the action. He wants people to get excited watching this flick, not fall asleep."

Rebekah completely ignored the big man and soon he was gone.

Glancing up at the clock she saw it was seven after three. Four o'clock was the deadline. She only had fifty-three minutes left. There were thirty-one pages left to write.

Suddenly it was eight minutes after three, her mind continued to wander. Then it was nine minutes after three and Rebekah had to force herself to concentrate on the computer screen and the script. Where did time go when you were finished using it?

Page sixty was completed. The script had thirty pages to go. There were forty-six minutes left. Thirty pages to write and forty-six minutes left in which to complete them.

Her fingers danced atop the keyboard, never stopping, putting dialogue into the mouths of the characters, describing fantastic vehicular chases and mass destruction to be enjoyed and consumed by the movie-going public.

She jumped when the cell door was again punched open.

"Pages," Joshua barked.

Momentarily taking the time to print what she had written, Rebekah did not lose a beat returning to the story.

"Mr. Warwick wants you to add another character."

Rebekah stopped cold.

"What?"

"A whore. You can call her whatever. Mr. Warwick wants the hero, Anthony, to screw her before he goes after the crooked cops. She can be some prostitute he helped while he was still on the force. Mr. Warwick wants her dead afterwards. Have her get shot then maybe she could fall out a window onto a car or something."

"But it makes no sense in the story for Anthony to stop to get laid."

"That's what Mr. Warwick wants."

"It's ridiculous," she insisted.

Joshua sighed heavily, retrieved his cell phone again.

Rebekah's eyes filled instantly with horror.

"No." She grabbed the big man's arm but he jerked it free.

"Yeah. She wants to argue."

Malcolm's muffled scream was heard through the concrete wall.

Joshua smiled, then turned and left.

Again she was alone in the cell, alone with the computer and the clock on the cold, gray wall.

Malcolm had never given Rebekah any indication that anything was wrong. She never once suspected there was a gambling problem.

Then the phone rang.

After he placed the phone back in its cradle, Malcolm pulled Rebekah away from where she had been cleaning the breakfast dishes and told her they had to go away. They had to go away fast and there was no time to waste. When Rebekah demanded to know what was going on, Malcolm just begged her to trust him.

But it had already been too late.

Men with guns were in their house.

"Pages," Joshua snapped, his voice booming off the block walls.

While the printer spit them out, he looked over Rebekah's shoulder.

"You put the whore in there like Mr. Warwick wanted."

"Yeah," she muttered. "And I gave her a big dick just for fun."

Joshua smiled, chuckled.

"I like you, darling. I really do. You got balls." He glanced down at his watch. "Thirty minutes left." He shuffled the new pages to the last. "Only twenty-four pages to go. You might just save that lousy son-of-a-bitch husband of yours for real."

On his way out Joshua snapped his fingers and spun around on the heels of his boots.

"Almost forgot. Mr. Warwick has another idea he wants put in the script. It's a scene in the beginning that shows Anthony and Carlito as kids, to help establish their lifelong friendship. Mr. Warwick believes it will better justify Anthony's revenge."

"I can do a flashback," Rebekah said, straining not to lose her concentration on the scene she was writing.

"Yeah, Mr. Warwick said no flashbacks. He wants you to go back and put it in the beginning of the story."

"The story already has a beginning," Rebekah snapped defensively, her concentration fully broken.

"Not my goddamn problem, darling." Joshua tapped the face of his watch. "Tick, tick, tick, tick…"

He slammed the cell door behind him.

On the car ride to Studio City, the big man Joshua informed Rebekah of her husband's outrageous gambling debts.

"He definitely owes the wrong people," Joshua assured.

The big man also informed her that Malcolm had put Rebekah's screenwriting skills up as collateral.

All the while Malcolm just sat quietly in the car, never denying a word Joshua spoke.

Joshua said Mr. Warwick was familiar with the two produced screenplays she had written. Although neither film broke any box office records and both were in different genres of film than what Mr. Warwick wanted her to write, he was excited to be working with someone of Rebekah's talents on his project.

When she tried to refuse, the big man shattered Malcolm's nose. Blood poured everywhere.

The building they stopped at was unassuming and rather ordinary. Inside, Rebekah was whisked away to the cell where she was given a one-page outline for the screenplay she was to write, and four hours in which to write it.

The clock started ticking at that moment and never stopped.

"Pages," Joshua barked at quarter to four. Rebekah had them printed out without missing a keystroke.

"Page eighty," he commented, collecting the pages. "Damn, darling, you are going to do it." He smiled. "It's nice working with a professional for a change." He rolled the pages up.

"Now, Mr. Warwick wants a really big finish. I'm talking colossal, lots of noise and gunplay. To ensure he gets his big finish, he wanted me to stress how serious he is about getting it." Joshua turned and called to someone outside the cell.

In the computer screen's reflection Rebekah saw her husband. He was bound to a wheelchair and pushed into the cell.

"Malcolm!" She immediately jumped up from the desk chair and moved toward him.

Joshua caught her with one big hand and slung her back into the chair.

"Plant your ass. You ain't done yet."

Terrified, Rebekah watched the man with the glasses and slicked back hair pull on a pair of rubber gloves. An ugly smile stretched across his face as he unbuckled Malcolm's belt and unhitched his blue jeans.

Malcolm jerked, screamed as best he could with his mouth full of bloody gauze.

"What are you doing?" Rebekah cried.

"Insurance, darling. Think of it as your epicenter of inspiration to do a really goddamn great, bang up job on the finale."

The man in glasses tugged at Malcolm's underwear and freed his penis. Malcolm struggled as his penis was placed between the gleaming blades of a pair of sewing scissors.

"It's a fair bet hubby here will be wiping his crack with a nub for the rest of his life, but if you don't want him whizzing through a little rubber hose, you best start hitting them keys, darling."

Fear kept her frozen stiff. She was momentarily unable to force her body to turn back around to the computer let alone concentrate on the final pages of the screenplay.

At last, when the man in glasses felt Rebekah needed a jumpstart to get back to work, he applied just enough pressure on the crisscrossing blades to draw a bead of blood.

Malcolm screamed wildly and went tense against his bindings.

Frantically, Rebekah spun around to face the computer. The words on the screen seemed foreign, as if they were written in another language. They meant nothing to her.

The clock showed three forty-eight.

Three minutes had been lost! Three precious minutes that could have been turned into script pages were now forever gone.

With ten pages to go, Rebekah wrote faster than she ever had. Faster, even, than she ever thought she was capable. Every second was vital and her fingers struggled to keep up with the ideas racing through her mind.

While she wrote, Rebekah was conscious of Malcolm's bloodied reflection staring desperately at her in the computer screen.

At three fifty-five she banged out the descriptive explosion of the warehouse where the band of crooked cops produced the illegal narcotics they sold.

Anthony, the story's hero, a rookie cop kicked off the force, mowed through the bad guys in a spectacular blaze of Hollywood firepower. Avenging the deaths of his family and lifelong friend, Anthony's aim was always on target and the bad guys always died a fantastic demise.

Joshua was behind her, reading over her shoulder. Malcolm was making silent noises like a hurt animal.

In their final showdown, Anthony fought hand to hand against the older cop who had once been his mentor, who turned out to be the cop overseeing the entire drug trafficking business and who put out the hit on Anthony's family and lifelong friend Carlito.

At three fifty-eight, Anthony delivered the killing blow that dropped the bad cop and brought the story to a satisfying conclusion. The dead were all avenged and the bad guys all dead.

"Make him get back up," Joshua said. She felt the big man's hot breath on her neck. "Have Anthony blow that son-of-a-bitch's head off with the shotgun he dropped."

Rebekah found the words she needed to create the violence she was instructed to write. She constructed a savage and grand struggle for the shotgun between the two characters. There was much violence, until the shotgun trigger was at last pulled.

"Oh, hell, yeah. That is nice, darling."

Daring to glance up at the clock, she saw the hour and minute arms slowly aligning into the four o'clock position.

Rebekah kept writing, her fingers jabbing the keyboard desperately to finish the final scene.

The second arm slowly made its final sweep around the clock face. Ticking past each second, it was responsible for creating all the minutes and hours and days that made up time.

Never stopping, her fingers pecked out an ending wherein the hero took one final look back at the destruction caused by his vengeance. It was like she was in a trance state, the words creating themselves through the movements of her hands and fingers. Her eyes kept straying to the clock in the final moments.

Unable to keep her eyes off the clock, Rebekah's fingers danced frantically while the clock's second arm ticked past the six. Ticking up past the seven and eight, the tiny arm crept higher.

At the nine there were fifteen seconds left. Pain was shooting through her wrists, up her forearms and into her shoulders, but Rebekah never slowed.

There were fourteen seconds left, then thirteen, and then twelve. The seconds suddenly seemed to be clicking by faster. Was it a trick of her eyes, or was time really speeding up, trying to cheat her?

There's no time, no time, never enough time to finish what you have to finish, never enough time...

Rebekah kept typing until the second arm swallowed up the remainder of her time.

"Stop," Joshua barked. "Pages."

Rebekah's fingers froze over the keyboard. Boiling hot blood pumped through her heart to all parts of her body, into her head. She felt dizzy, a little drunk. It was like the euphoria runners talked about after completing a race.

The last two words on the page were the most beautiful words she had ever written.

The End.

What was even more beautiful, those two words appeared on the bottom of page ninety.

Joshua took the pages and glanced through them. When he was satisfied he nodded to the man in glasses.

With a disappointed look, the man removed Malcolm's penis from the scissor blades and roughly tucked it back into his underwear.

Joshua looked from the script pages down at Malcolm in the wheelchair.

"This is a good woman you got here. She deserves better than you, asshole."

With an open hand, Joshua slapped Malcolm alongside his head. The blow sent the bound man tumbling sideways in the wheelchair. He crashed onto the dirty floor.

"Come on." Joshua and the man in glasses left the cell. The door slammed shut behind them, which was followed by the click of a deadbolt.

Rebekah rushed to Malcolm's side. She tried to right him in the wheelchair but it was too awkward and heavy. She pulled the bloody gauze out of his mouth.

"Why?" she asked quietly. Malcolm offered no answer. She sat on the floor, cradling her husband's head and crying for what seemed a long time.

Time seemed to no longer exist. The clock on the wall no longer had any meaning. She never even noticed when it showed a few minutes until five o'clock. She simply wept and caressed her husband's bruised and bloodied face, waiting for it to all be over.

"Break time's over, darling," Joshua said when he entered the cell. Two men Rebekah had never before seen entered with him.

Joshua took Rebekah by the arm and escorted her back over to the computer. The two men picked Malcolm up off the floor and righted the wheelchair.

"Mr. Warwick is very pleased with your script. You know, in this town, every-damn-body has a script poking out their ass. But not everybody is a screenwriter. Get my drift? It has truly been a thrill working with someone of your caliber."

"We paid you the script you wanted," she said in a quiet voice. "We want to go."

"You'll get to go, and all of hubby's debts will be cleared, but not just yet." He dropped a stack of papers nearly as thick as the finished script on the desk.

"Mr. Warwick has a few changes he wants you to make to the script. You know, stuff that will make it play better."

"What?" Rebekah asked. Her voice was barely a whisper.

"Mr. Warwick was really impressed with your script. It'll pull in some major players too. We're talking some big stars, a big director. It just needs a little rewrite, a little spit and polish."

"That was not part of the deal," Rebekah snapped. Her voice cracked.

"You know damn well that deals in this town are always changing, darling."

"I'm not going to do it," she retorted before she realized what she had said.

Without being told, the two men pulled the bloody gauze from Malcolm's mutilated right hand. Before she could stop them, Malcolm's scream pierced the air.

Her husband's pinky finger was cut free. It dropped to the floor and rolled a couple inches.

"You got two hours to finish the rewrite," Joshua said sternly. "And not a goddamn minute more."

The three men left the cell with Malcolm. Joshua pushed the cell door shut.

Rebekah sat for a moment trying to rationalize what just happened. Here entire body was shaking uncontrollably and she wondered if she was going into a state of shock.

It was like she was trapped in a nightmare world from which there was no escape.

Wiping the hot tears from her eyes, Rebekah breathed deeply several times.

She looked at the stack of notes Mr. Warwick had made concerning her script.

It would take her forever to read through all the notes before she could even begin applying them to the screenplay.

But she did not have forever. She had only two hours. That was a hundred and twenty minutes, seven thousand two hundred seconds.

That was not nearly forever.

The clock loomed overhead on the gray wall. It showed three minutes after five.

Three minutes were already gone, she thought frantically. One hundred and eighty seconds lost for all time!

There was an hour and fifty-seven minutes left. Soon, there would only be an hour and a half left, then only an hour.

The clock continued to click off the forever-lost moments of time, never stopping, never slowing.

Rebekah rubbed her burning hands and wrists. They hurt so badly.

Before any more time could be wasted, Rebekah began the rewrite.

Rosemary's Perfect Man

Working busily in the kitchen, Rosemary tended to boiling pots and the roast in the oven. A pinch of salt here, a dash of crushed pepper there; Rosemary had never considered herself much of a cook but she knew Bryan would love it.

The roast smelled wonderful. Turning the oven heat down she took two dinner rolls from their bag and placed them inside the toaster oven to brown. Although she had only been cooking for two a short time, Rosemary knew it was something she would definitely get used to doing. She found it so much more enjoyable preparing a meal for two rather than simply heating up a frozen dinner for one in the microwave.

Rosemary had always found eating alone to be regretfully dreadful. Her only dinner guests were people on the television and the only dinner conversation came from the voices creeping through the paper-thin walls from the adjoining apartments. Not to mention the city sounds that intruded upon the meal, the shouting from the streets below, the constant honking of car horns and roaring of trains and the never-ceasing wail of police sirens.

But all that had changed and Rosemary was cooking for two now, herself and Bryan. She smiled. Now there would be no more lonely nights eating a meal for one. She peeked in at Bryan. He sat on the sofa in the living room and watched the nightly news.

He was not like other men, Bryan, not like any of the other men Rosemary had ever known. Certainly, he was nothing like the lecherous Mr. Timmons, the building's maintenance man, who would ask embarrassingly personal questions while in her apartment fixing a leaky faucet or opening a clogged sink. Or like old Mr. Sawyer, the library's custodian, who spent his days with his head hung low, staring and peeking beneath the hemlines of the skirts and dresses of unwitting ladies.

He was absolutely not like Tommy Mosier, Rosemary thought with disdain while she mashed a pot of boiled potatoes. Bryan was not like the horrible Tommy Mosier at all. Not the same greasy hair or crooked smile or ugly laugh. Rosemary shuddered at the memory of Tommy Mosier, the memory of Tommy's rough hands and of how they pinched and groped and poked.

She slammed the pot of potatoes down hard on the countertop. Breathing deeply, she clenched her hands into tight fists until the memories were cast from her thoughts.

There was no point focusing on the unpleasantness of the past when the present was so promising, she decided, sighing heavily.

The potatoes were still lumpy. Putting a smile back on her face Rosemary continued her mashing until they were just right.

Bryan was a much better man than Rosemary had ever before known; much better than she had ever hoped or dreamed existed. Bryan loved her, cared for her. He listened to her, made her feel important. At night he held her in his big arms and made her feel safe.

A perfect man he was. She tasted the potatoes and decided to add another pinch of salt.

Polite, Bryan was, and intelligent and handsome and supportive. If only her mother had lived to see the day.

But she knows. Rosemary had long ago assured herself that mother watched over her from above. Mother knows and she is happy for Rosemary, happy that her daughter finally found a man in which to share her life. Someone who chased away the sadness and loneliness that came with every night.

Mother could stop worrying now that Rosemary had found a companion, her soul mate.

There was a knock at the apartment door.

"I'll get it, sweetheart," Rosemary called to Bryan. She wiped her hands on her apron before answering the door. She opened it the length of the brass colored security chain.

Two police officers stood in the hallway.

"Evening, ma'am," the older of the two officers said and tipped his hat. "I'm Officer Barton and this is Martz." The younger officer was to the side of him.

"Yes?" Rosemary could not imagine why two police officers would be at her door at dinnertime. Suddenly she thought of the rolls browning in the toaster oven.

"We hate to bother you ma'am, but we're talking to all the tenants tonight," Officer Barton said, sounding tired.

"Is something wrong?" Her brow creased with concern.

"We're looking for a missing person, ma'am," the younger officer, Martz, chimed in. He offered her a photo to look at.

The photo showed a young couple posing with their two children, one just a giggling baby on his father's knee.

"His name is Brandon Clark," Barton said after a moment. "He went missing about three days ago."

"Mr. Clark worked for the cable company," Martz offered. "His van was found parked a block down from your building. Mr. Clark had a number of service calls in this building Tuesday morning. The super remembered letting him in but didn't recall him leaving. Do you happen to remember seeing this man anytime Tuesday morning, or anytime after?"

Rosemary concentrated on the photo of the smiling family as if attempting to peer straight through it. Finally she shrugged her shoulders.

"I'm sorry but I don't ever remember seeing this gentle-man before." She offered a weak smile. "I don't even have cable television."

The younger officer jotted something down in a small flip notebook, and returned the notebook to his breast pocket when he was finished.

"Well," Barton started. "We do appreciate you taking the time to talk to us. Smells like we interrupted dinner. It smells pretty good too."

Rosemary blushed slightly. "It's no problem at all, officer." She took one last glance at the family in the photo before slid-ing it back through the crack of the door to Martz.

"He really has two beautiful children," she said.

"And one worried wife,' the younger cop said, taking the photo. "I can assure you of that."

"Thanks again," Officer Barton said tiredly, then turned to move to the next apartment down the hall.

Rosemary closed and locked the door.

Such a beautiful young family, she thought as she returned to the kitchen. So happy the man and the woman seemed, so much in love. How awful it must be for that poor woman not to know where her husband was, or if he was ever coming home. Those poor, beautiful children were without a father.

Her hands shook slightly. The smell of burning bread snapped her from her reverie. The rolls were burnt black in the toaster oven.

"Sorry, sweetie, but I burnt the rolls." She knew Bryan would not be upset at her for something so small. He never got angry with her, never said a cross word. She scraped the two rolls from the small pan into the garbage then went about preparing two plates of food.

So horrible, the nagging thought persisted, that those pre-cious children could be without a father for the rest of their lives. And the wife, the poor girl, to have found the right person, to have fallen in love and married and started a family, only to have her man disappear. She must be going out of her mind with grief. It was almost enough to make Rosemary lose her appetite.

She carried the plates into the living room and set them on colorful TV trays.

"I'll be right back with silverware and drinks," she told Bryan. Kissing his forehead she scooted the TV tray closer to where he sat on the sofa.

Collecting the needed utensils and pouring two glasses of milk, it occurred to her that the man in the photo resembled Bryan. They both shared the same curly brown hair and dark eyes, the same wide shoulders and muscular physique. Actually, they could easily pass for brothers.

Slamming the utensil drawer shut, Rosemary turned quickly, dropping one of the forks. Stopping herself, she took a deep breath and forced herself to calm down. It was a ridiculous thought. Bryan had told her their first night together that he did not have any brothers or sisters, no wife or any family at all.

He was just like Rosemary, alone in the world.

Picking up the fallen fork she pitched it into the sink and took a clean one from the drawer. It was time to chase all the silly ideas from her mind and enjoy the meal she prepared. No point in ruining a dinner she took so much time and effort to prepare.

Grabbing up two folded cloth napkins and the two glasses of milk, Rosemary put a smile on her face and joined Bryan in the living room. She beamed down at her man, her Bryan.

A reality show played on the television during dinner. It was one of the dating shows, where a dozen different prospective lovers courted one woman. Rosemary had wished longingly, just the week before in fact, to be on such a show. Now she watched it with Bryan's arm pulled around her, her head resting on his chest, near his heart.

After dinner, of which Bryan did not touch one bite, they sat and talked. Mostly it was about Rosemary's day at the library. Never once did Bryan interrupt, criticize or patronize her as she spoke. He silently sat and listened to every word she had to say, stories of late fees and loud talkers and cell phones and fellow employees who took long lunches. She talked until she was finished and Bryan sat quietly, unmoving, listening attentively, never interjecting his own thoughts or ideas into the conversation.

Finally, Rosemary took the dishes and glasses into the kitchen. After rinsing them off she stacked them in the sink until morning.

She showered and dressed for bed. She thought briefly about painting her toenails red, something she had never done before, to see if Bryan would like it, but it was getting late.

A recap of the earlier news broadcast was on the television when she returned to the living room. Finding the remote she turned the television off. With much effort she pulled Bryan off the sofa and dragged him down the tiny hallway to her bedroom.

On the floor of her bedroom she undressed him. The uniform she had washed and pressed that morning before going to work she folded neatly on wire hangers and placed in the closet.

She padded into the bathroom and brushed her teeth. When she returned she carried the bottle of cologne she bought at the supermarket after work when she picked up the roast for dinner. She smeared a dab on either side of Bryan's cold neck and some on his still chest. Inhaling the musky scent deeply as she recapped the bottle, she returned the cologne to the shelf she had designated for Bryan's toiletries in the medicine cabinet.

Turning off the bathroom light behind her, Rosemary moved toward her bed and turned down the sheets. With a little extra exertion, she got Bryan into a sitting position, leaning alongside the bed.

Rosemary climbed onto the bed. With legs tucked beneath her, she grabbed Bryan underneath each arm and hefted his muscular body onto the mattress.

"I think I'm feeding you too much," she said, giggling like a schoolgirl as she caught her breath.

While situating Bryan on the bed and getting his body under the covers, one of his hands passed gently across her breast. Calloused and rough from work, but gentle, Rosemary felt the electricity from his simple touch, and her body reacted. Just like their first night together. It seemed so long ago but it was only three nights ago, Tuesday night.

"I love you." She kissed Bryan on the forehead and then on the lips.

Reaching for the switch on the little lamp on the nightstand, Rosemary filled the room with darkness. But it was no longer a lonely darkness or a sad darkness.

Rosemary crawled under the cool sheets. She snuggled into Bryan's strong arms and nestled her head atop his broad, still chest.

Within minutes she was asleep in Bryan's comforting embrace. She was no longer afraid or lonely. Now she dreamed when the darkness enveloped her. She dreamed of starting a family with Bryan one day soon. She dreamed of two beautiful children, one just a giggling baby, and of her smiling in a photo with them, her family, and of coming home after work and cooking for them, cooking for her family.

Clyde

Hefting the box of dishes up the front porch stairs, Shelby Stevens set the box down hard on the porch decking. Although there were only four steps up to the porch, the effort sent little jolts of pain up her legs and back. She rested momentarily on a solid box marked "Books" in black marker.

It felt wonderful to be off her aching feet, if for only a few minutes. At least it was not a hot day. The heat would just make her feel more nauseated than she already felt. She rubbed the swell of her belly affectionately.

Bruce came out the front door with the two movers and stopped when he saw his wife resting.

"You okay?" he asked. He kissed her sweaty forehead.

"Holding out," she answered with her best attempt at a "don't worry about me" smile.

"We got the bed put together if you want to lie down for a little while," he offered. "You'll have to go through some boxes to find the pillows but a rest might do you good."

"Too noisy," she said. "I'll sleep well tonight."

Suddenly, Shelby jumped when she felt something rub against her leg.

Bruce laughed.

"Looks like we just met our first neighbor," he said with a smile.

The tortoiseshell colored tabby brushed alongside Shelby's bare legs.

She reached down and scratched the feline behind its ears. The cat purred affectionately.

Bruce squatted down to pet the tabby but the cat moved away from him, hiding behind Shelby's legs for protection.

"Well, he definitely likes the ladies. Should I be jealous?"

"He's got a collar and a tag," Shelby said, scratching around the tabby's neck until she could see the silver tag affixed to the collar.

It simply read Clyde.

"His name's Clyde," she said. The cat purred louder as she continued to scratch him around his neck.

"He must belong to somebody around here," Bruce said. He wished his wife would stop petting the animal so it would go away.

Suddenly, a barrage of wild barking and the scampering of nails on hardwood floor filled the quiet afternoon air. Clyde jumped protectively into Shelby's lap as Wilma, Bruce's Pomeranian pup, bolted fiercely through the open front door.

"Ouch," Shelby said loudly. Clyde's claws dug into her bare flesh. The cat was terrified of the little dog. She picked the tabby off her lap for relief, surprised at how heavy it was. It weighed a good ten pounds at least, if not more. It squirmed and struggled in her grip, hissing and clawing at the barking dog.

"Knock it off, killer," Bruce said and swiped the puppy up in one hand.

"That's not the best way to be introduced to the new neighbors," he scolded Wilma.

Unable to calm the cat, Shelby dropped it to the porch. Landing on its four paws, the cat took off running around the side of the house.

"Oh, Jeez, hon, you're bleeding." Bruce was looking at the scratches on her legs.

"I'm fine," she said. Standing, she took Wilma from Bruce. "I'll put her back in the bathroom."

"I can take care of her," Bruce offered.

"No," Shelby snapped a little too sharply. "I'll put her back in the bathroom then go clean up. You stay with the movers."

Bruce knew when to keep quiet and he did.

After securing the little dog inside the downstairs bathroom, Shelby went up to the master bedroom. There she found the packing box containing the first aid kit. She poured peroxide on the cuts and wiped them clean, then put bandages over the worst of the cuts.

She was exhausted, totally wiped out. The bed, even without sheets, pillows and comforter looked very inviting.

Kicking off her sandals she spread out on the bare mattress.

Before succumbing to exhaustion she heard a tiny scratching coming from somewhere in the room. At first she thought it was the puppy, scratching on the bathroom door downstairs, but she was too far away to hear that.

Looking around the room she found the source of the noise.

Clyde, the tortoise-shell tabby, sat on the outside sill of one of the bedroom windows.

The animal was still, just watching her now that she had noticed it.

She knew the cat did not mean to hurt her. It just reacted instinctively to the barking dog.

She wondered how the cat had gotten up to the second story window. Her thinking was foggy as she started to drift off to sleep.

There was the tree alongside the house, she realized. Clyde could have easily climbed the tree to get to that particular window.

Before finally falling off to sleep, Shelby wondered how the cat knew which window sill to climb onto to find her in the big house.

* * *

When Shelby awoke it was still light out, but the sunlight was waning. She looked at her watch. She had been asleep for a solid three hours.

The window where the tabby Clyde had been perched when she fell to sleep was empty. Now she wondered if she had only imagined the cat there, looking in at her.

Pulling herself up off the bare mattress, Shelby padded into the bathroom. After relieving herself, she slowly made her way out to the hallway.

In the hallway she heard the tapping of fingers upon a keyboard. The repetitive tapping got louder and louder and was then followed by a parade of garbled curses.

She poked her head into the room Bruce had chosen for his office.

"Does the cursing help?" she asked and yawned.

"It helps me," he said, looking up at her. "Sleeping Beauty still looks tired."

"Sleeping Beauty feels like hell. She's hungry too."

"I was going to wake you soon and see if you wanted to eat. I lost track of time fooling around with this damn thing." He pushed the keyboard away.

"What are you hungry for?" he asked, getting up from his desk. The office, like the rest of the house, was full of un-packed boxes.

"Pizza," Shelby answered quickly. "With extra cheese, pepperoni and mushrooms."

"You got it," Bruce said, kissing his wife on the cheek.

While Bruce went down to the kitchen to order the pizza, Shelby wandered into the baby's room. The walls were plain but soon they would be painted in bright colors. Now was not the best time for a move, what with the baby due in three months, but Bruce could not pass up the promotion he had been offered.

She imagined what the room would look like once she had it ready to welcome the new baby. She imagined the smell of the new baby and the sounds of the infant filling the house. It was going to be so wonderful.

Rubbing her belly, Shelby turned and went downstairs to join her husband.

* * *

From the fence in the backyard, the tabby sat quietly and watched the house.

The little dog paced on the other side of the sliding glass door. Watching the cat outside, it scratched at the glass and barked wildly.

Outside, the cat never moved from its perch. It just sat and watched the little dog inside the house.

* * *

"Shut up, Wilma," Bruce snapped again.

"Just put her outside," Shelby said. She rubbed her temples. The little dog's constant barking was making her head throb.

"She's really not an outdoor dog," he said in a quiet tone.

"She is tonight," Shelby said. Her words were sharp with irritation. Opening the sliding glass door she shooed the little dog out onto the back porch.

* * *

Haunches raised, the tabby watched the little dog bark ferociously from the edge of the concrete porch slab, and waited.

* * *

"What are you doing?" Bruce asked, not believing what his wife had just done.

"Getting some peace and quiet, that's what I'm doing."

"What if she gets out of the fence?"

"She'll probably be too scared to step off the porch. Let her bark her little head off then we'll let her back in for the night."

"So can I expect you to put the baby outside if he's crying and you don't want to listen to him?"

Shelby just glared at Bruce a moment but did not respond to his remark. Before either could say another word there was a knock at the door.

"The pizza," she said.

Bruce simply threw up his hands in defeat, grabbed the checkbook and went to answer the door.

Rather than a pizza delivery person, an older couple stood smiling on the other side of the door when he opened it.

"Hello," Bruce said, taken aback.

"Welcome to the neighborhood," the woman said. "I'm Cleo Watkins and this is my husband Aubie."

The man next to her nodded but kept quiet.

"We saw you moving in but didn't want to get in the way. You're not eating dinner are you? We don't want to interrupt." The old woman looked past Bruce into the house, as if casing the place.

"No. We're waiting for food but it's not gotten here yet. Please, come in, I'm Bruce Stevens." He welcomed the Watkins into his home and shook the older man's hand.

"Honey," he called to Shelby, who appeared from the kitchen with plates and napkins expecting to find dinner, not old people standing in her front room.

"Honey," Bruce started, making a face to his wife the old couple could not see. "This is Cleo and Aubie Watkins."

"We live two doors down," Cleo said, stepping over towards Shelby. "We've lived in this neighborhood nearly thirty years, haven't we, Aubie?"

The old man just shook his head quietly.

"You're pregnant," the woman said with delight. "Do you have any other children?"

"This will be our first," Shelby said with a smile, setting the plates down on the coffee table.

"How wonderful it will be to have children running around this neighborhood again. Most have grown and moved away, haven't they, Aubie?"

Again the man nodded in silent agreement with his wife.

"We don't want to take up a lot of your time tonight. We just wanted to introduce ourselves. We live two houses down if you ever need anything."

There was another knock at the door.

"Excuse me," Bruce said and answered the door.

This time it was the pizza delivery boy.

Cleo Watkins took the opportunity to look around the house. Shelby noticed the woman paying particular attention to the wall at the bottom of the stairs near the front door. She leaned over to her husband and said something in a quiet voice. Shelby strained to hear without looking obvious. It sounded like the woman said, "You can't even tell." The man just nodded his head.

"Oh, well, we are disrupting your dinner now," Cleo said and moved toward her husband.

"We appreciate you stopping by," Shelby said with a bright smile. "You'll have to introduce us to the rest of the neighborhood."

"Absolutely," Cleo said as she and Aubie made their way to the door.

"I told you they would be eating dinner," the woman whispered to her husband just loud enough for Bruce and Shelby to hear.

When they were gone Bruce shut the door and snapped the deadbolt lock.

"Jesus," he said and Shelby burst out laughing.

* * *

After dinner Bruce stacked the dishes in the sink while Shelby found the bed sheets and pillows and made the bed.

When he was done in the kitchen Bruce lumbered into the bedroom. His body ached from moving furniture and heavy boxes all day. He had one more day off from work to unpack before he had to start the new job.

Entering the bedroom he heard the blast of the shower coming from the bathroom.

Shelby stood under the hot spray, the water massaging her tired body.

Then she felt a different type of massaging upon her neck and she giggled.

"You're tense, lady," Bruce said, kissing his wife's neck.

"What are you doing?" she playfully asked when she felt Bruce's hands cup her breasts.

"They're getting huge," he said, leaning against her body in the hot spray.

"They're for the baby."

"That's not fair." He gently caressed the tips of her breasts until the nipples grew hard.

Shelby felt Bruce's hardness pushing against her.

Turning to face him they kissed under the spray. Bruce kissed his way down her neck to the hardened nubs of her nipples.

Moaning, Shelby moved away from him.

"What?" he asked.

"Not now," she said quietly. She smiled, caressing the side of his face.

"It's all right," he said, but Shelby knew he was disappointed.

"It's just that I'm all fat and ugly."

"You're all fat and beautiful," he responded and tried to kiss her again, but she backed away from him.

Frustrated, Bruce kissed her cheek and got out of the shower.

* * *

Bruce was reading a horror paperback when Shelby came to bed. It was marvelous to slide between the sheets after the shower.

"So what did you think of the Watkins?" she asked, trying to determine if her husband was angry at her.

"I thought they were like the creepy old people in that movie *Rosemary's Baby*," Bruce said without looking away from his novel.

"The old lady said something really strange to her husband when you were paying for the pizza. She said, 'you can't even tell.' What the heck do you think she meant by that?"

"Who knows," Bruce said, dog-earing the page he was on and closing the book. "She's a loon and her husband's got no balls so who cares."

He flipped the lamp next to the bed off and rolled over.

It wasn't long before Shelby forgot all about the Watkins and that Bruce was mad at her and fell off to sleep.

* * *

After waking early, Shelby made coffee and put away dishes and cookware in her new kitchen while Bruce unloaded boxes and scooted furniture.

Drinking her morning mug of java Shelby noticed how quiet it was in the house. It was quieter than their old house in Portland.

"Oh, crap." Padding over to the sliding glass door, she opened it and stepped out onto the concrete porch. The back yard was silent and still in the early morning sun.

"Wilma," she called out, looking around for the little dog.

The concrete was already hot under her bare feet. It was going to be a scorcher, she thought, wondering where Bruce's beloved little pup could have gotten.

The corner of the porch was stained a brownish color she had not before noticed.

It seemed to trail off into the grass. Shelby followed the trail around the side of the house, over to where the air conditioning unit sat.

Bruce heard her scream from inside. He bolted out the back door and found his wife hunched over and throwing up in the backyard.

* * *

"I am so sorry." Shelby's eyes were watery and red from crying.

"I forgot about her too," Bruce responded in a cool, even tone.

"What happened?"

"She was mangled." Bruce drew a glass of cold water from the tap and drank it fast. He was sweating from digging the hole and burying the puppy in the backyard.

"Could a coyote get in the backyard?"

"How should I know?" He slammed the glass down on the counter top harder than he had anticipated. "Look," he said, attempting a calmer tone, "I'm sorry. I'm just upset. As long as you're okay everything's fine. Let's forget it and try to get a little more unpacking done."

Bruce moved out of the kitchen and went upstairs to unload more boxes in his office and the spare bedroom.

Shelby felt completely alone. She felt as if she had in some way betrayed her husband by leaving the little dog outside and forgetting about it.

She sat at the table in the breakfast nook staring out into the backyard.

Clyde the cat was on the back porch. He rubbed his body against the sliding glass door screen a couple of times then wandered off.

* * *

During the days when Bruce was putting in long hours at his new job, Shelby busied herself doing what she was able to make their new house a home.

She worked long hours in the baby's room, painting the walls and putting up borders, assembling the new crib and changing station.

When she rested she sat out on the back porch to get a little sun. Even on the hot days she tried to sit out for a half hour or so, just to be outside the confines of the house for a short while.

The tortoise shell colored tabby was almost always outside, as if waiting for her to come out and sit.

Eventually Shelby set out a water bowl for the cat, it was so hot. Then she bought a cheap bag of cat food and fed it daily outside.

Sitting in her lap, the cat purred as Shelby scratched behind its ears and neck, and petted its long body.

Petting the cat helped to calm her nerves. The cat returned her affection by nuzzling in her arms and falling asleep in her hold. It was nice to have something around the house that returned her affections.

* * *

Walking from his office and reading the Blackie file, Bruce came to a dead stop in the upstairs hallway.

In the nursery, the fat tabby with the nametag that read Clyde was curled in a ball in the middle of the baby's crib.

"Get the hell out of there!" Bruce raged, swatting the cat with the file.

On its feet instantly, the cat hissed at Bruce and pawed at the air.

"Don't you dare, you little bastard!" Bruce whacked the cat on the head with the file.

"Stop it!"

Shelby was at the door to the baby's room. The cat jumped from the crib and scampered away, darting between her legs.

"What in the hell is that mangy cat doing in the house, in the goddamned crib?" Bruce was enraged.

"He shouldn't have been in the crib." She went to the crib. The bare mattress was covered in cat hair.

"That damn cat shouldn't be in the house!" he screamed.

"That damn cat pays more attention to me than you do," she hollered back. "He shows me some affection."

"I try to show you affection and you push me away!"

Shelby's face clouded with disgust and disappointment.

"You be seven and a half months pregnant and tell me how affectionate you feel like getting, you bastard."

She stormed out of the nursery without another word.

Bruce just stood in the baby's room by himself for a long moment cursing silently before returning to his office, angry and frustrated.

* * *

A plate of food was waiting for Bruce in the microwave. He was running late again.

It wouldn't be dinner if it didn't have to be reheated, she thought.

Clyde was rolled in a ball on the floor in the living room. The television played softly so there was some sound in the house.

Shelby had called her sister April earlier and talked for almost two hours. Her younger sister was still not married, free to live her life as she wanted.

Although she never came out and said it, Shelby was jealous of her little sister. To be single again, she thought, and not put up with the moods of a spouse or the changes of your body with a new life growing inside it.

That was selfish, she knew. It was just her out of whack hormones working on her. She tried not to dwell on such thoughts. She loved Bruce and he loved her and they would see their way through any hard times they were having.

* * *

When Bruce arrived home the house was dark and still. He found Shelby asleep on the couch.

The television was the only source of light in the house and its glow cast ever moving shadows all about the front room.

Looking down at his wife, Bruce felt horrible for all the friction lately. His job was pushing too hard and with the baby coming, it felt like his life was speeding right past him and closing in on him, all at the same time.

Shelby was the only one who ever cared for him, supported him. His family had never been there for him when he was putting himself through college. But Shelby always stuck by him.

Moving toward the couch to kiss his wife, he suddenly lost his balance and fell forward when he stepped on the cat on the floor.

Bruce had not even seen the feline rolled in a ball on the floor in the room's darkness.

The tabby screeched as Bruce fell on Shelby's legs on the couch.

Shelby was startled awake when her husband's weight fell upon her.

"What?" she snapped as she woke, disoriented and irritated.

"That goddamn cat is still in the house," he spat. "It almost killed me!"

"God, you never get tired of it, do you?" Shelby got up from the couch.

"What?"

"You start the day fighting and you finish the day fighting."

"But I'm not…"

Without a word, Shelby shuffled up the stairs.

From the couch Bruce heard the door to the spare bedroom slam shut.

* * *

Bruce found his plate of food in the microwave. It looked like it had already been reheated once and did not look very appetizing.

He brushed the contents of the plate off into the waste can and dropped the plate in the sink.

From the refrigerator he took a bottle of beer and drank most of it in one long gulp. Finishing the beer he threw the empty bottle away then retrieved another.

It was late but he was too wound up to try and sleep, especially by himself. The few times he and Shelby had not slept together during their six years of marriage had been restless nights. Bruce had grown accustomed to Shelby's warm body being next to his when he slept.

At the bottom of the dark staircase he stopped.

That goddamn cat could be on any of these steps and I wouldn't know it, he thought. Flipping the stairwell light on the brightness revealed no cat. Shelby had probably taken it into the spare bedroom with her.

Bruce ascended the stairs and made his way to his office. For a split second he thought about going in to Shelby to apologize, but decided against it. Tonight was not the time. It could wait until morning if he even bothered with an apology at all.

A spotlight of moonlight lit a patch of carpet in the baby's room. The cat Clyde slept curled in a ball in the center of the spotlight.

"Little bastard," he mumbled under his breath then went to his office.

* * *

For thirty minutes Bruce looked at charts and graphs and records but he could not focus well enough to actually get anything accomplished.

He still was not ready for bed and his stomach was grumbling. Plus, he could use another beer.

Looking through the stack of files he could not find the Blackie file. He searched through his file cabinet then strained to remember where he last had it.

This morning, he remembered. It was the file he used to hit the cat in the baby's room.

He looked around, knowing he laid it somewhere on his desk.

"To hell with it," he grumbled and pushed away from the desk.

Getting up he grabbed the empty beer bottle and flipped off the light when he left the room. Another beer and a frozen dinner and he would be able to fall asleep on the couch.

In the dark hallway he moved carefully. Reaching for the light switch at the top of the stairwell he stopped.

The cat was still asleep on the floor in the baby's room.

"I'll get rid of that goddamn cat first thing this weekend," he mumbled quietly. His words were a little slurred. The beer had given him quite a nice buzz on an empty stomach.

On the fourth step down the world was yanked out from underneath Bruce Stevens. He flailed his arms uselessly and fell into the darkness.

* * *

The sudden commotion woke Shelby from her sleep. She ran from the spare bedroom at the end of the hallway to the bedroom she shared with her husband.

"Bruce?"

Their bedroom was empty.

Switching on lights she saw the scatter of loose papers all over the stairs and an empty file lying open.

At the bottom of the stairs she saw her husband.

"No!"

Rushing down the stairs, leaning all her weight on the oak railing, Shelby neared the foot of the staircase when she stepped on a sheet of paper and lost her footing.

She fell hard down the last three steps and landed on the unmoving body of her husband.

Pain filled her whole body and the world spun wildly around her. Before it all went black, Shelby thought of what an odd angle her husband's head was twisted.

* * *

Everything around her was a blur. She recognized doctors and nurses by the way they were dressed, but the words that came out of their constantly chattering mouths formed a thick slush in her ears.

At one point she recognized her sister, April. How nice it was for April to come visit but why was the girl crying?

Crying and talking, April chattered on like the doctors and nurses but all Shelby could think about was the void she now felt inside her. Something was different, missing. She felt like a part of her was gone, dead.

Bruce was gone; she knew that. The image of his grotesquely twisted head staring at her haunted her dreams.

Shelby dozed in and out for several restless hours, her brain lost somewhere between sweet dreams and horrid nightmares.

* * *

April did not want to leave her sister, but the doctor told her there was nothing she could do for Shelby. He wanted to keep Shelby at least another night and then maybe release her the following morning.

The nurses found the keys to her older sister's house and helped give April directions to the place.

Twice on the way April had to pull over because she was crying. How could this have happened? How could Bruce be dead? How could Shelby have lost the baby?

None of it seemed fair or made any rational sense.

When April found the house it was getting dark. She hefted her suitcase out of the trunk and dragged it inside.

Another bout of tears came when she looked around the empty house, the brand new house Shelby and Bruce had just moved into.

The house should be filled with their voices and soon with the crying of a newborn. Shelby should be running around being a mother and wife, not lying in a hospital bed.

April slumped onto the couch and sobbed for the life that had been horribly stolen from her older sister.

She jerked suddenly when a furry body rubbed against her legs.

"Give me a heart attack," she said and wiped her eyes before petting the cat.

The tabby purred and frantically brushed alongside April's hand and legs.

"God," April said aloud. "You must be starving."

Wiping the last of the tears from her eyes, she got up and went into the kitchen.

"Where's your food bowl?"

The tabby meowed loudly, as if actually attempting to answer.

"Okay. I'm sure that means something in cat-anese, but I don't understand it." She looked around the kitchen, thought where she would most likely put the bowls if it were her cat then found two empty bowls in the corner of the breakfast nook.

"Now we're cooking. Where's your food, Ace?"

As if understanding, the cat darted toward the pantry door. It stretched its long body toward the pantry door's knob and meowed.

"This is going to be extremely creepy if I find your food in here."

On the bottom pantry shelf April found the bag of dried cat food.

The tabby circled her and meowed wildly until the food bowl was filled. Crunching the food loudly, the cat was immediately in the food bowl eating. April took its water bowl over to the sink and filled it with fresh water.

Listening to the cat attack its food, April realized how hungry she was. She wondered when she had eaten last. Not since arriving and going straight to the hospital early that morning.

April inspected the refrigerator, then the freezer. Quickly she decided she did not want to wait for something to cook, not even in the microwave.

"I'll be back in a jiffy," she said to the cat. The cat paid her no attention and continued to eat.

Walking through the empty house April grabbed her purse, found her keys and Shelby's keys.

Swinging the front door open April jumped and let out a scream when she saw the old woman on the front porch.

The old woman jumped too. She had a hand up as if ready to knock on the door.

"Good Lord, girl," Cleo Watkins said, catching her breath.

"Sorry, I didn't know you were there," April said, composing herself quickly and letting out a little giggle.

"I just saw the lights on and I thought Shelby was home."

"The doctor thinks he might let me bring her home tomorrow. Oh, I'm April, Shelby's sister."

"Glad to meet you. I'm Cleo Watkins, from a few doors down."

The women were silent a moment before the older woman began to speak in hushed tones.

"Horrible what happened to Bruce," the old woman said slowly. "Nice fellow. We saw the ambulance this morning. It was such a shock. And losing the baby is tragic. I have a friend who volunteers a couple hours a week at the hospital. She was working when they brought poor Shelby in this morning." Cleo fell silent again.

"It happened here before," Cleo said quietly.

"What happened here before?" April asked. She had heard about the kindly but kooky old Mrs. Watkins from her sister. Under the circumstances, the old broad was spooking her.

"Accidents." The old woman looked over April's shoulder, as if expecting to see someone else standing and listening to them.

"Jake and Minnie Katz, the people who lived here before, they had an accident. Jake took a fall down these same stairs. He had his head go right through the wall here." Cleo nodded at the wall.

"God, what happened?"

"Like I said, they called it an accident." The old woman was silent for another moment before continuing.

"I know what did it."

Like a snake, the tabby hissed ferociously and both women jumped.

"Knock it off," April said, looking down at the feline. When she looked back up old Mrs. Watkins was already off the front stoop and quickly making her way across the front yards to her house.

"Crazy people," April muttered. After making sure she had both sets of keys and checking the cash in her wallet, she finally left her sister's house.

She did not notice when the cat named Clyde slid out the front door and merged with the night's darkness.

* * *

Cleo drank another glass of wine. Her hands were shaking terribly and the glass clicked off her teeth when she drank.

Aubie sat in the TV room and watched the news.

"Lord, it can't be," she whispered, pouring another glass of wine and drinking it quickly.

She had to start dinner, but she was still shaken.

How in the world could that be the same cat?

"It couldn't," she mumbled to herself and finished the wine.

Although she was still nervous, she had calmed enough to begin dinner. The wine was making her feel a little light-headed.

She took an onion and a green pepper from the crisper in the refrigerator and began slicing them on the cutting board next to the sink.

Outside the night was completely black.

How could it be the same cat?

There was no way possible it could be the same cat, her mind repeated.

Cleo Watkins was lost in her thoughts and the mechanics of chopping when the night came to life. It howled like a newborn demon birthed from the bowels of hell and its eyes glimmered and its sharp teeth threatened to swallow her up.

The night creature slammed into the window above the sink with enough force to rattle the panes and make Cleo jump. The serrated cutting knife jumped too, and bit a deep burning gash into her thumb. The blade only stopped cutting when it found bone.

* * *

Approaching the house April saw her sister's cat out on the front stoop. The cat was pacing back and forth, rubbing its side against the front door.

"Oh, hell," she muttered, carrying the Chinese take-out up to the door.

"When did you sneak out?"

The cat meowed loudly.

"Let's get inside." April found the house key and opened the door.

Two houses down Aubie Watkins rushed his wife to the emergency room.

* * *

Shelby was confused. When April said she was taking her home, Shelby thought her little sister was talking about the house over on Pinecrest.

But that was crazy, Shelby thought. They had moved out of that house nearly twenty years ago, right after Dad died. That house was in a completely different state.

Shelby did not immediately recognize the house they finally pulled up to. It looked familiar, but it was not the house in Portland. It was not the house she and Bruce had bought right after they were married.

But then she remembered that Bruce was no longer there. Bruce was dead. So was the baby.

There was so much to do, so much to take care of, her mind rattled. Shelby had a funeral to take care of, two actually.

Would her unborn child be placed in a miniature casket next to the father?

Her head hurt and there were so many thoughts. All she wanted to do was lay down and never get back up.

April helped her to her bed.

* * *

Shelby stirred when she heard her sister's voice.

She was comfortable where she was and basked in the wonderful feeling of warm life resting next to her belly.

"Get out of here!" April snapped.

Still half asleep, Shelby was awake enough to see her sister push the tabby off the bed from where it had been laying next to her.

"Get out!" April practically screamed.

The cat sat at the bed's corner defiantly, staring at the younger woman.

"Go," April said. She reached out to push the cat off the bed corner.

Hissing, Clyde sprang. The tabby lashed out and put three short burning cuts across the top of April's hand.

"You little…" April snatched her hand back. The cat bolted off the bed and ran out of the room.

"Don't," Shelby said in a tired voice.

"You don't need that damn cat sleeping in the bed with you."

"Clyde's my baby."

April did not know how to respond to her sister's remark. Shelby was on a lot of different medicines, and her head was in a really bad place. There was no point in arguing with her.

"You need to get up and eat," April finally said.

"I'm not hungry."

"You need to eat something. Maybe just some soup, something light."

"I really couldn't eat a thing," Shelby said and rolled over, pulling a pillow over her head.

"Fine." The doctor had told April to try to get her sister to eat something, but if Shelby did not want to eat, there was no point in trying to force her. Their mother would arrive in a day or so and April figured she would have a better chance of getting Shelby to eat and respond.

April went to the upstairs bathroom and drew a hot bath. She poured bath oil in the steaming water. With all that was going on, and all that needed to be done, the bath would no doubt help relieve some of her stress.

When the tub was full she turned off the faucets and slid out of her clothes.

The water enveloped her in a cocoon of warmth. She lay her head back and put a wet washcloth across her eyes.

Her muscles relaxed in the heated water. The stress of the past few days seemed to momentarily melt away in the bath.

If she wasn't careful, she thought, she could easily fall asleep in the tub.

The house was quiet; the world was quiet.

Then slowly, the door to the bathroom creaked open.

"Shelby?"

Taking the washcloth off her face April sat up in the tub.

No one was there.

No one except for the cat Clyde sitting on the bathroom floor, staring at her.

"What the hell do you want you furry little freak?"

April splashed the cat with water to scare it away. But the cat just sat there. It did not even flinch when she splashed it a second time.

What kind of cat didn't run away deathly afraid of water, April wondered.

The tabby leaped up onto the vanity next to the tub. Its big body knocked over bottles of shampoo and conditioner, and sent containers of medicine bouncing into the sink and onto the floor.

April suddenly became very afraid. The cat continued its walk to the edge of the vanity.

"No!" April screamed and tried to jump from the tub.

The tabby's big body gave the hair dryer just enough of a push to send it splashing into the tub.

April's body shook spasmodically in the electrified water, her skin cooking, turning black, and then she fell limply into the water when the socket's fuse finally blew.

* * *

Shelby awoke when Bruce turned on the bedroom's overhead light. The light was bright and burned her eyes.

"Were you planning on sleeping all day?" He sat a tray down next to her on the bed.

"What time is it?" She yawned and stretched.

"It's past noon. I thought you might be hungry."

The food on the plate was Bruce's attempt at cooking, a fast food burger and fries.

She smiled.

"You shouldn't have gone to all this trouble."

Bruce laughed.

"Look," he knelt down next to the bed and took her hand into his. "I know we've been going through a tough time and I've been being a big ass, but I'm sorry. I'm losing my mind with this job and I'm worried about you and, I guess I've just been handling it badly." He kissed her hand.

Without a word she leaned toward him and their lips met.

The longer their lips held the more passion seemed to boil between them. Shelby felt her husband's hands on her body. His touch sent her skin prickling with excitement.

The tray of food fell to the floor but neither noticed.

Shelby moaned as her husband kissed a hot path down her neck to the tips of her breasts.

Her nipples stiffened as his lips sucked them in, licked them.

But something was different.

It was hurting.

Bruce's tongue was different. It hurt when he ran it across her. It was rough, like wet sandpaper.

"Stop," she whispered, but he did not stop. His flickering tongue quickened.

"Stop," Shelby said aloud, shaking herself awake.

The tortoise shell colored tabby named Clyde was hunched over on her chest. The cat's head was burrowed beneath her nightgown.

It was licking feverishly at the seeping milk from her breast.

"God, stop it!" she screamed and sat upright.

Startled, Clyde cut a dozen burning furrows into her stomach until it untangled and freed itself from her nightgown.

"Goddamn you," she screamed, lashing out while cradling her bleeding flesh.

The cat jumped on her hand and bit down fast and hard. Shelby tried to shake the cat loose, but it held tight, ripping at her arms with its claws and biting more ferociously on her hand.

Finally the weight of the cat slid over the side of the bed and released her arm. Clyde bolted out of the room.

* * *

In the master bathroom Shelby wiped her bleeding stomach with a damp towel. Blood continued to ooze from the slashes across her skin.

A feeling of nausea overwhelmed her but she fought it back.

God, she could still feel the cat's tongue lapping at her breast.

She had to get the cat out of the house. It was feral, possibly suffering from some kind of disease like rabies.

It hurt to walk. The lacerations burned when her skin moved and stretched with each step.

In the hallway she called out for her sister. Nothing but dead quietness responded.

"April, are you here?"

Slowly, Shelby made her way down to the spare bedroom.

The air in the hallway was heavy and smelled like overcooked meat.

The spare bedroom was empty and so was Bruce's office.

On her way downstairs Shelby noticed the smell was coming from the bathroom down the hall.

"April?"

The door creaked open.

"Are you in here?"

April's charred body lay in the still water of the tub. The bottom half of the clear plastic shower curtain was melted over her blackened husk.

Shelby choked back a scream and stumbled out of the bathroom. When she bumped into the oak railing behind her, the scream ripped free from her lungs and filled the house.

Shocked into action, she raced down the stairs.

She had to get out of the house, get the police.

Her mind was screaming so many directions at her, where to run, what to do, she ran blindly into the darkened front room.

Banging her shin on the coffee table, Shelby hunched over in pain.

The darkness came alive then, howling and hissing. Long furrows of pain were dug deep into her back and neck.

Reaching behind, Shelby grabbed the tabby by the collar and tore it from her back.

She heard it hissing and moving around in the dark room.

Frantically feeling for the coffee table like a blind person, Shelby found her way to the couch. Once she was on the couch she moved over and found the lamp on the end table next to the couch.

Light momentarily filled the room like a bolt of lightning before Clyde sprang and knocked the lamp to the ground. Instantly bursting, the bulb died and returned the house to blackness.

Shelby sat still on the couch too afraid to move. The scratches on her arms and stomach and back were stinging and she felt blood pouring from them. Her shin throbbed in pain.

Clyde struck again, biting her bare feet and tearing at the flesh around her ankles.

Kicking out ferociously Shelby managed a solid kick to the tabby's stomach that sent the cat retreating.

The cat was crazy, wild. She had to get out of the house now.

Everything was suddenly quiet and still. Straining, Shelby could not hear the cat moving around. All she heard was the thunderous beat of her own heart.

Before the cat could attack again Shelby bolted toward the kitchen. Frantically she slapped at the wall switch to ignite the overhead light. The fluorescent fixture took a moment to blink to life.

Find a weapon, her mind shouted. Find a weapon to beat the cat off, kill it.

There was a howl behind her. Shelby turned in time to see Clyde leap from the kitchen island counter directly at her.

The cat's weight slammed into her, its claws tore wildly all over her body.

Pushing the cat away, Shelby reached desperately for the utensil drawer for a weapon.

Pain erupted up her leg and she shrieked as the feline sank its sharp teeth into the back of her bare leg.

It was the tabby's turn to cry out when the tines of the fork jabbed into its back. It scampered away.

With precious moments to find a better weapon Shelby jerked open the cutlery drawer. Inside she found a heavy meat cleaver.

She turned to see the tabby perched upon the island watching her every move.

"I thought we were friends, Clyde," Shelby said in a soft, even tone. "I thought you were my little buddy."

The cat never moved, even when Shelby took a short step forward. It just watched her with wide, curious eyes.

"But you killed everybody, Clyde. You killed Bruce, my baby, April." She took another small step toward the island counter.

"I bet those aren't the only people you ever killed, are they, Clyde?"

A low guttural growl rolled from deep within the feline's throat.

"I didn't think so." She moved closer. "I bet they're just the tip of the iceberg, right Clyde? I have a feeling you've been doing this for a long time."

Never losing focus, the cat watched intently as Shelby took another small step forward.

"What are you?" Shelby whispered.

In the darkness, the cat's eyes seemed to glow demonically, staring at her unblinkingly.

The weight of the cleaver felt good in her hand.

"What in the hell are you," she screamed and lunged toward the cat. The cleaver swung down quickly.

The cat yowled when the cleaver sheared off the tip of its tail and embedded itself deep into the counter top.

Slashing claws filled her face when the cat leapt, cutting her lips, nose, tearing across her eyes.

Shelby screamed and pulled at the cleaver while the cat bit deeply into her forehead.

When the cleaver finally pulled free Shelby lost her balance and fell backwards with the tabby straddling her head. Losing her balance Shelby slammed onto the tiled floor hard, with her head snapping off the floor and bucking the cat loose.

Everything was still for a moment before the white-hot pain filled her body.

With shaking, bloody hands, Shelby felt around her side and found the center of the pain. The cleaver was biting deep into her side where she had fallen on to its blade. Blood poured over her trembling fingers.

The tabby was there, staring down curiously at her. Clyde's eyes were focused just on her. It seemed like the cat stared down at her for an eternity.

The last sensation Shelby Stevens felt before she died was that of the tabby poking its mouth into the open wound and lapping feverishly at her seeping blood.

* * *

"Hurry up, slow poke. You got a lot more to move." Reggie Perro waved at his wife from a second story window.

Sure, Mitzi thought. Hurry up. We just started and Hercules wants everything unpacked in a couple hours so he can get the truck back early.

Mitzi walked several boxes into the new house before finally having to sit down on the front porch steps for a break.

They only had about an hour of sunlight left, she thought. It was getting darker earlier with autumn on the way. Autumn was her favorite time of the year.

Lost in the thought of what the big front yard would look like once all the trees had shed their leaves for winter, Mitzi jumped, startled by something brushing along her legs.

"What?" Reggie asked, huffing toward the moving truck from the house for another box.

"A little friend," Mitzi said. She petted the tortoise shell colored tabby along the back. It began purring immediately at her touch.

"He's a big one," Reggie said and reached down to pet the cat too.

The tabby jerked away, hid on the other side of Mitzi, away from him.

"He prefers the ladies," Mitzi said with a laugh.

"And he's extremely homophobic too," Reggie said and laughed.

"Oh, god, Reggie, look. Someone cut off the tip of his tail. What kind of monster would do something like that to such a sweet kitty?" She scratched the cat behind its ears.

"He belongs to someone," Reggie said, noticing the collar and tag around the tabby's neck.

Gently, Mitzi continued to scratch behind the tabby's ears so she could get a look at the tag.

"It just says 'Clyde,'" Mitzi said, looking up at her husband.

The Drive-In Slasher

His wristwatch showed six forty-seven, exactly two minutes past the last time he checked it. Dennis Mackek wiped a hand across his sweaty forehead. It was late in the day and still too hot. Eyes roaming the streets, Dennis continued to cruise. The sun had not even gone down yet and already the sidewalks were rolled up in this town.

"Damn it." He smacked the steering wheel with an open palm. He was beginning to think that somewhere along the way, since leaving Kearny, he had taken a wrong turn. It had been a very damn bad wrong turn into Nowheresville.

Dennis began thinking of other options, not that he had many. There was always the option to just go to the drive-in alone and find a girl already there. He did not care much for that prospect. Girls very rarely went to the drive-in movies by themselves, especially to the all night spook show. Mostly they only attended with a date or in the company of friends.

Finding someone already at the drive-in was tricky too because there were always so many people around, all those prying eyes looking around, seeing things they should not see.

Too risky, Dennis finally decided. Continuing his search he turned the car down another quiet street in the town square. All the businesses seemed to be abandoned.

"This place is like a ghost town," he mumbled. It was too quiet. The quietness seemed to make the world even hotter. Dennis flipped on the AM receiver to put some noise in the air. The cool chords of Link Wray & His Ray Men's 'Rumble' spilled from the speakers.

"That's it, dad," Dennis said and moved his body with the music. Tapping his fingers on the steering wheel, he felt like a predator, an alligator swimming around the swamp on the lookout for some trouble to get into.

Finally, the sun began its lazy meltdown as the day drew nearer to night. Soon it would be gone, gone and waking up the other side of the world. When it was completely gone, darkness would settle in. When it was dark, it would be time for the show to start.

Tapping along with the music, Dennis figured it would be good and dark by quarter to eight. What day was it, he wondered. What month? The summer was getting away from him. Eventually he would have to head down south for a spell, then out west where the drive-in theaters stayed open all year round.

A funny noise interrupted both Link Wray and Dennis' train of thought. When he heard it a second time he realized it was his stomach grumbling.

The time was ten minutes to seven. Dennis had not eaten a bite all day. He drove through from Kearny last night and stopped only long enough to grab a few hours' rest on the shoulder of the highway and then later to fill the gas tank. Eating had completely slipped his mind.

He hated to stop the hunt, especially since he had not yet found a girl to accompany him to the all night spook show. But he knew if he was going to eat it had to be now. By the time he got to the drive-in, he would be too busy to stop and eat.

An Everly Brothers tune came on the radio. Dennis followed the lonely street away from the quiet town square and eventually came to a crossroad and a greasy spoon.

To Dennis, the diner looked like a dirty train car. The neon sign on its roof cracked and sizzled and said simply, Chuck's.

He pulled into the lot and parked next to a sky blue sedan. The only other vehicle in the lot was a rust bucket jalopy.

Like the rest of the town, nothing much exciting was happening inside Chuck's Diner. A man and a woman sat in a booth eating their blue-plate specials and an old man sipped from a coffee mug on a stool up at the long counter. Not much of a dinner crowd.

The spinning ceiling fans did little to cut through the pungent odor of the millions of cigarettes that had been smoked in the belly of the diner. Dennis took a back booth and slid in next to a window.

Smudge marks covered the menu but Dennis knew what he wanted and did not bother to dirty his hands. He had eaten at dozens of places like this one over the summer since graduating school. A grilled cheese sandwich with a side of fries and strong, black coffee was almost always an easy magic trick for any halfway competent hash-jockey to make appear.

Dennis caught his breath when the waitress wandered up to the booth.

"What'll it be?" Her words were lacking any real concern. The look on her face said she was bored to tears in this place.

Even with her hair rolled up in a bun, and little make-up on, the girl was a real looker. She had beautiful, round blue eyes, high cheekbones, full lips and the apron tied around her waist did little to conceal the magnificent figure beneath.

"If you're dumb, just point to something on the menu, sweetie. I have to be able to write something down to give to Wally." She half turned toward the grill where a grease spattered man in horn-rimmed glasses stood holding a spatula dripping with lard.

Snapping to attention, Dennis smiled. He liked this girl. She had a fire in her and she did not appear to be much older than he was.

"A grilled cheese sandwich with fries and coffee."

"We can put a scrambled egg in it for five cents more," she said without making eye contact.

"Scrambled eggs in the coffee?"

It was her turn to smile. "Cute." She gave him the slightest wink then went off to give the cook the order and get the coffee.

He watched as she poured the coffee. She had a grace that was wasted in this grease shack. She brought the mug to him, setting it on the table. Wisps of steam danced atop the coffee's black surface.

"Are you new in town?" She looked down at him as if studying him like a science experiment.

"Just passing through."

"Me too. Do you always drink coffee on hot summer days?"

Smiling, he replied, "It helps me stay awake. I'm headed over to the drive-in for the all-night spook show."

Suddenly, her interest in their conversation seemed genuine. "Really?"

"Yeah, really. You want to come along or something?" Dennis knew that was stupid before he finished saying it. Too many people had seen him. The cook could probably identify him later to the police. Now he was letting everyone know where he was headed for the evening.

"I'd love to go," she said excitedly. Her face relaxed, losing some of its hardness, and her eyes sparkled. "I love the drive-in and the movies. Oh, the movies. I've loved the movies for as long as I remember. But I haven't gone since I moved here. I don't know anyone and I don't have a car. It's awful to go to the movies by yourself anyway, don't you think?"

"It's the worst," Dennis commented quietly. He hoped no one in the diner could hear what the waitress was saying.

She regarded him a moment with a raised eyebrow. "Are you being serious about the movies or are you just putting me on?"

This was the moment of truth, Dennis thought. He could tell her he was just joking and apologize, look like a heel and go on, or he could take full advantage of this sudden turn of good luck and grab the brass ring.

Outside the shadows were growing long. The day was cooling off, getting dark.

"Like I said, it's an all-night spook show tonight," he said with a grin. "I never miss the spook show."

Behind the waitress a bell was slapped. She turned to retrieve the order. When she returned she put his plate on the table in front of him.

"If you're serious, I get off at seven-thirty."

Dennis looked at his watch.

"You'll have plenty of time to eat your dinner and drink another cup of coffee."

"Sounds like a plan." Inside, he felt as if a great weight had been lifted off him. Relief washed over him and for the first time all day he could afford to relax a little.

Turning away the waitress stopped and spun back around. "Can we run by my place before we go? I'd like to get out of this get-up and wash up."

"Whatever you need," Dennis assured her with a nod. Feeling good he took a big bite from his grilled cheese sandwich.

* * *

On the way to the boarding house where she rented a room for five dollars a week, Dennis learned the waitress's name was Angela King. He also learned she was nineteen, and she had moved from Dillsburg less than a week ago. Angela was only working at the diner until she earned enough money to buy a bus ticket to California.

"Hollywood or bust," she said and giggled. "Since I've been a little girl I always wanted to move there and be a big, famous movie star." She batted her eyes seductively like Marilyn Monroe.

"You might have what it takes," Dennis said, pulling to the curb in front of the boarding house.

He waited in the car and listened to the radio while Angela washed and dressed for the movies.

When he saw her coming down the walkway he got out of the car to open the door. His jaw nearly hit the sidewalk when he got a good look at her.

Her hair was out of the bun and flowing down her back. She wore a thin blouse and a skirt and stockings. There was a slight hint of garter riding high on her thigh and peeking from beneath the skirt line. He was careful when he shut the door behind her.

Dennis Mackek felt like the luckiest guy in the world. He moved around to his side of the car and slid in. Pulling the door shut he revved the engine. With a screech the car sped away from the curb.

* * *

It was Saturday night and Pipp's Auto-Vue was swinging. Stars filled the dark sky while atomic monsters lurched across the giant screen. Deep in the passion pit of Pipp's, there were steamed up car windows as far as the eye could see.

Roland Pipp was locked in his office counting the quarter-a-carload take on the nearly sold-out dusk-to-dawn 'Shiver-and-Screech' horror show. Pipp hoped all the little punks came up for air long enough to drop some change on snacks between shows.

While giant cicadas overtook the city of Chicago on the giant screen, Dennis Mackek had his lips practically welded onto Angela King's. His hands made a move under her skirt. His fingers glided over the garter belt and gently slid under the silky stocking for a touch of warm flesh.

Playfully, Angela pushed him back with a sly grin. "You are a naughty boy."

"I just know what I want." He leaned toward her but Angela put a hand up to stop him.

"It's getting awful hot in here," she purred.

"Yes it is."

"I need to cool down. I'm thirsty." Her tone was playful and her words tickled his ears.

"Thirsty?"

"Thirsty." Her lips brushed against his momentarily, a promise of things to come.

"What does my little waitress want?" Dennis wasn't agitated because he knew this was all part of the game.

"I don't care. Surprise me."

"Surprise you?"

"Yeah. Then maybe I'll surprise you." She licked her red lips.

Grinning, Dennis got out of the car.

The night air was fresh, especially after the stuffy confines of the car. Walking to the snack bar he still could not believe how lucky he was to have found Angela. Had he not stopped at the diner for a bite to eat before the movies, he would have had to come to the theater alone.

Pushing through the glass door and entering the concession, Dennis enjoyed the heady feeling of his evening's good fortune.

With the first movie of the spook show still in full swing, the snack bar was empty. A skinny guy no thicker than the mop handle he leaned on stood and talked to an older woman in a hairnet reading a newspaper behind the counter.

"Says here the Sky-Way in Kearny was the sixth drive-in the creep hit this month. He slashed that poor girl to ribbons."

She folded the newspaper to look at the skinny guy. "Kearny's only a hundred and fifty miles away."

Dennis stepped up to the counter and waited to be helped.

The woman in the hairnet noticed him and put the newspaper down. "Can I help you?"

"How about two Cokes and a small Buttercup."

The woman went about collecting the order.

"You heard about this 'Drive-in Slasher', boy?" the skinny guy asked Dennis.

"As a matter of fact I have."

"According to the paper, he only strikes during the all-night, dusk-to-dawn spook shows. He could be out there right now." The skinny guy nodded out toward the lot.

"Heaven's sake, Link, stop it. You sound like a damn fool." The woman set the sodas on the counter top.

"But he could be, Lorraine. Like you said, Kearny's only a hundred and fifty miles away."

"If you don't stop running your mouth, Link, I'm gonna fill it with that filthy mop of yours." She set the popcorn next to the sodas and totaled the order. "That will be thirty-five cents."

Dennis went into his pocket for the change. His fingers moved around the switchblade knife to retrieve a quarter and two Indian head nickels.

"Why do you suppose he strikes only during the dusk-to-dawn shows?" Link asked, much to Lorraine's chagrin.

"Maybe," Dennis started, dropping the coins on the counter top, "it takes him a while to do what he needs to do to his victim, and a regular double feature doesn't give him enough time." Smiling, he collected his order and left.

"That was one strange fella," Link said when Dennis was gone. Loraine snapped her paper open.

"It says here," she began reading, "that another body was found at a theater in Dillsburg about a week ago. But that body had been strangled and they don't think it's by the same guy who's been cutting up the girls."

Link thought a moment, then said, "Well, Dillsburg is only ninety miles away."

* * *

Dennis was thinking about Angela, and about the switchblade in his pocket, and of all the fun things they were going to do before the spook show ended. He opened the car door with a big, easy grin.

Immediately he noticed the silky stocking draped over the head rest of his seat.

Angela sat with her legs crossed. Both were bare from the tops of her thighs down to the tips of her red painted toes.

Hurriedly, Dennis got into the car and set the drinks and popcorn on the dashboard.

"Do you like what you see?" Angela purred.

"It's a surprise all right."

Angela moved across the front seat and they embraced. The temperature began to rise inside the car as they kissed passionately and steamed up the windows again.

Carefully, without alerting Angela, Dennis fumbled into his pocket to procure the switchblade as they got more comfortable in the big front seat.

Angela swung one leg over and straddled Dennis's lap. She ground her pelvis into him and felt his immediate reaction to her moving body straining to be freed.

There was the silent flip of the switchblade snapping open, but Angela seemed not to notice. She smothered Dennis with her full lips, her fingers running through his hair.

In her deep, sensuous voice, she tickled his ear with a whisper. "Are you ready for your surprise, naughty boy?"

"I'm ready." Slowly, so as not to catch her attention, he brought the knife up behind her. It was inches from her throat.

His grip tightened on the handle.

With one swift movement he would cut her, feel her body tense and go limp in his arms.

"Good," she whispered in his ear.

With one quick movement Angela had the stocking draped over the head rest twisted around his throat and pulled into a tight knot. She pulled both ends with all her strength.

Choking, Dennis tried to buck the girl off him, but she had him pinned down. He tried to grab her but she put one end of the stocking garrote in her mouth and then with her free hand she violently poked him in the eyes.

The sudden blast of pain caught him off guard and he stopped struggling and dropped the knife.

Angela pulled both ends of the stocking savagely and the world began to go black as Dennis Mackek felt flushed and horribly dizzy. His mouth struggled to suck in air, fill his lungs, but like a fish out of water he was suffocating. The last thing he saw was Angela leaning toward him. Her eyes were incredibly round and blue, like pools of water.

The last thing he felt were her lips pressed heavily upon his.

* * *

When Angela leaned back, the boy was dead. Her body was tingling all over and it took her a minute to catch her breath.

"That was real good," she said, brushing her hair out of her face. She kissed Dennis on the cheek then slid off his lap. Her bare foot found the fallen switchblade on the floorboard. "What the hell?" She picked it up.

"Unbelievable," she said to herself, agitated. "I really know how to pick them." She looked at Dennis. "I read about you in the paper. You've been stealing my thunder, daddy-o."

Dennis remained silent and still. His dead, glazed eyes were staring blankly up at the outdoor screen.

"I guess you were going to use this on me, huh?"

Dennis continued to stare unblinking, mouth agape.

"Jerk!" She slammed the knife to the hilt into him again and again and then finally left it jutting from his chest when the worst of her rage passed.

"A girl can never meet anyone decent anymore!" After she calmed down, Angela went about sliding her stockings back on and straightening her clothes.

After the third movie she made her way to the ladies' restroom and whipped up some quick tears. A blonde teenager named Wendy Baker found her and asked what was wrong.

Angela explained to the girl that she and her boyfriend just had a terrible fight. Angry, he pushed her out of the car and left her, and now she had no way home.

Wendy tried to calm her down, tried to get Angela to stop crying. She told Angela that she and her boyfriend Frank would be more than happy to give her a ride home. When Angela tried to decline the offer, Wendy assured her it was no problem because she was tired of the horror movies and was going to have Frank take her home soon anyhow.

Grateful for the ride and the help of strangers, Angela left with the teenaged couple. One last glance proved that no one was the least bit interested in the dead boy hunched over the front seat of the black sedan in the back corner of the lot. No one even noticed he was there.

* * *

The following day, Pipp's Auto-Vue Drive-in Theater made the headlines. The Drive-in Slasher had struck again, this time claiming his first male victim.

Pecking Order

Wallace Parker had no idea what type of bird he was hazily staring at. He had a limited knowledge of the feathered species, not knowing if it were a sparrow, finch or linnet. By its down of brown feathers, Parker deduced it was neither cardinal nor blue jay. Songbird or lovebird, Parker had no clue. If it were yellow it could be Tweety bird from the cartoons. Its little body hopped along on fragile looking stick-like legs.

It was close enough to snatch, just grab up in one swift motion, Parker thought. If only his arms were still capable of movement.

The edges of the world around him were soft and out of focus. His mind was fuzzy, as if wrapped in thick wool. The last remnants of the unconsciousness from which he had just awoken were still clinging to him, still attempting to drown him into its forceful, dark embrace.

Parker was horribly thirsty. His throat was dry and cracked. The only taste in his mouth was that of sour blood.

Pecking flesh from Parker's open hand, the bird scuttled back a step, awaiting a reaction from its prey. Tiny black eyes watched closely the hand for some kind of responsive reaction while it ground up and swallowed the plug of flesh.

Forget snatching the bird, or even swiping it away, he realized with dread. He could no more strike at the feathered beast than he could flinch from what should have registered in his nerve endings as a burning, stinging pain. His body was paralyzed, devoid of movement and feeling. The little beak burrowed deeper into the hole it already made and gnawed away more bits of his flesh.

I must be dead, Parker concluded grimly. That's why I cannot feel anything, not the pain in my still body or even the little bird pecking into me. That's why I cannot move my body, scare it the hell away. I'm dead. It's the only answer that makes any sense.

What the hell happened to me?

Blinking, the world slowly started revealing more of itself to Parker in sharper focus. He saw trees, limbs swaying softly above him in the breeze. Blindingly bright beams of sunlight penetrated through the entangled tree limbs and sat warmly on his face.

With all his strength he slowly lifted his head from the musty ground. The effort resulted in an electric explosion of hot pain erupting within his skull. His brain was suddenly on fire, seared by the livewire of movement.

Parker tried to grab his head and cradle it until the horrendous pain subsided, but his arms remained immobile, completely unresponsive to the directions of his brain.

The pain crashed throughout his head, throbbing behind his eyes and filling his ears. A wave of nausea passed over him. He tried to ride out the wave and keep from losing his stomach. Acidic bile burned in the back of his throat. If he lost his stomach he feared he would be unable to roll to his side, and would drown lying there.

Sucking in air, Parker found it difficult to breathe too deeply. Capable of only short gasps of breath, he imagined that if he were capable of currently feeling anything below his neck, it would no doubt be the hot, lancing pain of a broken rib tearing into his lungs.

What the hell happened to me, his mind cried out over and over again. The only sound around him was the breeze blowing in the trees. Something moved nearby in the dry leaves. He hoped it was just a dead branch falling to the earth. He could not contemplate the idea of an animal, a wolf or even a curious squirrel or snake, finding him in such a vulnerable state.

But what if it is a hiker, or a hunter, his mind countered. What if it was someone who could help him?

Withstanding the intense pain, Parker twisted his head gently to one side, attempting to get his bearings.

The day was bright and clear, the swollen sun hot and brilliant. Except for the rustling spring breeze there was no other movement. No wolf or squirrel or hiker or savior.

When he could no longer hold his head up, Parker let it fall to the ground with a wince and a sigh.

As best as he could determine from his limited vision and quick glance around, he was lying in the shallow ditch that ran along the side of the narrow forest road.

Oh, God!

A thundering filled Parker's head. Slow and steady, the rhythmic thumping was suddenly all around him, swallowing him completely. After several moments that felt like lifetimes, he realized the thunder in his head was his heartbeat. It beat even more frantically when, in short, staccato bursts, little snatches of memory suddenly came to him with a lightning blast fury.

Parker had left nearly a week ago, been on the road six days so far. He just up and walked out on Annie and her two kids late one night after the comfort of gentle lovemaking had relaxed Annie into a deep sleep. A shadow slipping quietly away into the night he fancied himself, as he took his waiting rucksack and stole into the night. Annie slept unknowing. Parker had been with the woman and her kids Samuel and Becky for almost two months. It was time to break camp, find another town to explore, secure another warm bed in which to rest and see how the world had changed since the last time he checked.

Parker loved the adventure of strolling into a new town, of meeting new people, expanding upon his vast collection of stories and characters.

If ever queried as to his trade, Parker reveled in telling folks he was an adventurer, a dreamer, a journeyman on a quest to collect a treasure of varied experiences and stories. A teller of tales, he shared his life lessons, changing the intimate details to entertain the collected listeners and to ensure his beer mug never went empty. He swore he would one day write a book, put all he had seen and touched and smelled and felt and tasted to words on paper. One day he would.

Besides the stories which made strangers his friends, Parker had a gentlemanly demeanor which helped secure him the bed of a lonely woman during his stay in whatever town he wandered into. The broken hearts of many a lonely woman were enticed by Parker's exciting tales and they usually offered freely a warm place for him to lay his head.

In less than two years Wallace Parker had made temporary homes in more than thirty small towns in just the southern part of the country alone. Odd jobs helped pay his way along when required and provided whatever funds needed when the night tempted him away.

The few possessions he owned were kept in the ragged rucksack he carried slung over his shoulder. It amounted to little more than a couple pairs of underwear and socks, a cigar box full of photos and a dozen notebook journals and pens. Wherever it was now, Parker had no clue.

To no avail, he tried to move his hands. He struggled to make movement in his legs, but they remained still. The best he could do was the limited movement of his head, which resulted in the terrible pain; the sucking, short breaths of air and the occasional, involuntary blink of an eye.

He remembered walking down the forest road. Cool but bright, the sun had felt wonderful on his face that morning when he awoke and resumed his trek.

The last ride he could recall was with the young couple headed to the Gulf to visit family. At noon they stopped at a roadside diner for lunch. Although Parker appreciated the lift, he left his road companions and opted to hike the back road spiraling through the green forest into the hills.

"That's what I'm into experiencing," Parker offered as explanation and extended his hand in goodbye. With a paper bag full of cheeseburgers and canned sodas stowed in his rucksack for dinner, Parker made his way up the dirt road cutting through the thick forest.

Feigning courage when it realized Parker was paying it no attention, the little bird hopped atop his forearm. Two quick bobs of it head and the bird had another morsel of flesh clenched in its beak. Parker watched horrified, straining his eyes, but was unable to scare it away.

A tidbit of trivia flashed across his aching mind. It was something from a TV game show, some minute, obscure fact his mind had filed away then suddenly regurgitated it for no apparent reason other than to torture him further. It was something about birds eating twice, if not three times their own body weight every day.

Was it possible the little bird would continue to peck on him until it had consumed, say, a whole finger? Would it continue to eat, simply gorging itself because he was an easy meal?

If only I could yell out, scream a curse and scare the despicable little creature away, Parker thought. Maybe someone close by, enjoying the clear sunny day, would hear the scream. God, anyone, his mind shrieked as he tried to cry out. The effort was lost before it even escaped his lungs. Just breathing was effort enough. He could forget crying for help. This was pure insanity.

Very few cars took the dirt road through the forest. he noticed when he started his trek. The cars that did pass raced at such dangerous speeds on the curvy and narrow road, Parker was less interested in obtaining another ride than staying out of the way of the rocketing metal beasts.

More pieces of the puzzle painfully revealed themselves and fell neatly into their place.

With a quick flutter of wings, the little bird hopped across his broken, shattered chest. Parker strained to see. Sunlight radiated out from around the bird where it stood atop the jut of a bone threatening to poke through both his flesh and shirt. The tip where the bird perched was stained a dark crimson. Parker realized it was probably better he could feel nothing below his neck.

In the distance of his memory, he recalled the blaring music that caught his attention. It seemed an intrusion, an attack, on such a peaceful, lovely day.

He turned to see who was coming and the music turned into the screeching of tires spinning out of control over an uneven dirt path. It registered, much too late to do him any good, how out of control the vehicle seemed. In an instant his eyes locked with the eyes of the driver and Parker froze where he stood.

Swerving, trying not to skip off the road and bounce out of control between the trees, the driver smashed the brake pedal. Screaming across the path, the car sounded like a freight train and blazoned a trail directly toward Parker until it was upon him. The metal monster smashed into him, its grill appeared in a flash like an open, gnashing, hungry mouth. The mouth shredded and tore savagely into Parker's body.

His eyes filled with a lightning bolt of brightness then he felt nothing as his body was tossed limply to the side, discarded like a crumpled drinking cup. Then the darkness swept him away.

Parker winced at the vivid recollection, as if he felt it all over again, when his body of soft flesh and bones connected with the out of control vehicle. Flushing red, he felt his face go hot and another wave of nausea washed over him. He struggled to keep his stomach down as another splash of bile burned the back of his throat.

When he was calmer, Parker moved his head slightly, rolling his eyes around. To the best of his vision, he was unable to locate the car that hit him. Which meant the driver had been able to navigate his car away from the trees.

Which meant the driver had fled, Parker's blood splashed on his grill, leaving Parker behind like a ruined bag of shattered bones and mangled meat. Human road kill.

At that moment, he felt like an insect squashed on a window screen, smeared along the network of wired squares but not yet dead, completely aware of its broken, battered body strewn about.

Maybe the guy stopped, checked him out and thought he was dead. Parker had to think of something to settle the anger clutching his heart. If the guy stopped, it would have been easy to think Parker was dead. It was possible too that the driver went to get help. Cell phones would be of no use in the thick, hilly forest. It was only a couple miles back down; close enough to the diner to call for help.

His heart sank. Try as he might, he could not dismiss the idea that the driver simply panicked and fled.

Parker could curse only in low grunts, his mind reeling in the grotesque reality of his situation. Silently he wished a horrible, lonely death on the person responsible for hitting him and leaving him for dead. Clearly, he could imagine the car swerve too near the sheer edge of the hilly dirt road, rolling, tumbling down the drop to the little valley near the Interstate. Parker delighted in the blossom of brilliant orange and red flame he saw in his mind. When he concentrated, he could see the driver of the vehicle trapped inside, his body cooking as he pleaded for help and forgiveness. Parker enjoyed the pleading, the screaming wildly for forgiveness as the driver's insides ignited in the lapping flames.

Lost in the vividness of his vindictive daydream, he hadn't noticed the little bird pecking at his neck until it hopped onto his chin.

Regarding Parker with a curious tilt of its head, its black eyes cast the reflection of a man. Parker recognized immediately the man reflected in the bottomless black orbs, saw the look of fear on the man's face. Before the fear could gestate into panic, the bird's head plunged forward, its beak pinching a generous gouge of flesh from Parker's bottom lip, tearing it free.

Unlike the nips taken from his open hand and arm, even his neck, pain registered like a lightning blast in Parker's mind as the bird pecked again at his torn lower lip.

With all his effort Parker shook his head, hoping to dislodge the bird from his face. Fluttering its wing fiercely for balance, the bird kept its perch. It hopped from Parker's chin onto his torn lip, its tiny claws squeezing and securing onto the bloody flesh.

Desperately Parker attempted to blow a puff of air at the creature in hopes of scaring it away. Something so simple had become nearly physically impossible. The breath caught in his throat, threatening to choke him.

The familiar feeling of nausea overcame him again.

With quick, rapid jabs, the bird began pecking at his face. Ragged jags of flesh were torn free of Parker's cringing face. Then his nose, the tip ripped open. Parker felt the warm wash of blood on his face as it poured from his new wound.

God, help me!

His face was burning, stinging with pain as the bird continued its feverish plucking. All the while his once healthy body lie still, unable to move or flinch or react in any way to the determined little bird's vicious attack.

Frantically, Parker tried to spit, tried to force his tattered lungs to expel a blast of air, twist some sort of frightening noise from within to stop the bird's siege on his face.

Two short, quick hops was all it took and suddenly the bird was perching on the bloodied tip of Parker's ruined nose.

The world was silent. The little bird's tiny eyes registered no emotion, just the reflection of raw fear.

Parker yearned to scream out, laugh even, at this absurd situation. It was like some stupid joke, man versus killer bird. Only the inevitable punch line scared Parker to death.

The little bird moved quickly then.

A sharp pain gouged into his left eye, as if the business end of a ballpoint pen had been thrust deep into the socket. A slight, sorrowful wail emitted from his throat. He sounded like a wounded dog. Parker shut his eyes but not before the little bird again plunged with its sharp beak.

Agonizing pain shot through his head. Against all the pain Parker shook his head, desperate to throw the demented beast free of his face. If luck could just be on his side, the little bird would fall in his mouth and Parker could grind it up, chew the vile little monster into a lump of bloody feathers. Imagining spitting the dead bird from his mouth, he shook wildly but still the bird held tight, determined not to be knocked from its perch.

When the effort of movement finally made his head go numb, Parker felt the beak pecking ferociously at the membrane of his eyelid. Eyelashes were savagely plucked like unfortunate worms in the sadistic early bird's assault.

His mind screamed for the pain to finally come to an end, but his mouth only pushed out short, strained breaths. Grunting, Parker kept his lids shut as tightly as possible but the savageness of the little bird persisted.

Eventually, Parker felt his eyelid succumb to the mad, frantic pecking and ripping. It tore away like loose skin around a fingernail, in one hot, sizzling piece.

Now, his attacker was completely visible. There was no escape. He could no longer shut it out. Hiding behind the darkness of closed eyes was no longer an option. Parker had damn few options left.

The attacker bobbed its head, then lurched forward, plucking and pecking and pulling until Parker felt his left eye burst under the unrelenting assault. His sight vanished instantly and his socket filled with a warm fluid that poured down the side of his face. He actually felt the head of his attacker working inside his own, its beak cutting deeper into his skull like scissors. The pain erupted in ever widening waves.

Suddenly, a car came racing up the wooded path. Startled, the little bird flew away.

Music pounded all around him as the car neared. Salvation! Parker's mind rejoiced. I'm saved! I'll be found and taken to a hospital. Saved.

He listened intently, waited to hear the car stop. His mind was screaming the joys of rescue as the car took the last bend and approached quickly.

What a story this day is going to make, he thought. Who would believe it? Who cared? It was the kind of survival story that would sell a million books, easy.

The music began fading as the sound of the roaring tires sped away.

Soon, it was quiet again.

The breeze blew through the reaching trees, rustled the limbs and leaves.

Something moved nearby. No doubt a dead branch falling to the earth.

Lying in the ditch, the sun on his face, his head thumping in rippling waves of pain, Wallace Parker silently prayed to God. He shut his right eye, his ravaged left eye no longer capable of sight, and prayed to die. He thanked the Lord for what he believed was the wonderful life he was given, prayed forgiveness for any of the lonely women whose broken hearts he had taken advantage and then explained how never in his life he had wanted anything more than his current desire to be released from his earthly pain and suffering.

He prayed intensely for a long time, blocking out everything around him, his ruined lips moving slightly in his silent prayers.

As if in answer to his prayer, Parker heard the celestial flutter of angel's wings. It sounded as if an entire flock of the cherubic entities were descending from heaven to take him in their warm, loving embrace, to lift him up, to help him shed his broken vessel and enter into the next life. He opened his eye to look upon their peaceful, heavenly countenances when he felt their soft, feathery wings caress his ruined body.

Parker's heart skipped a beat but, refusing to stop, cruelly continued to pump life.

The little bird had returned. This time it brought friends.

Jack Fright

Maggie Anderson scooped another handful of snow and packed it onto Old Jack's bulging midsection. "Let's give you a big, fat belly this year," she said to the snowman, packing in the white flakes.

If only the children were still here, she thought, smiling. Her gloves were soaked through and her hands were wet. The early morning wind stung her face and she turned away from the freezing gusts until they passed.

She used to love watching the children on Christmas morning, their excited little faces aglow, their little bodies rushing downstairs to see the sparkling Christmas tree and the drift of colorfully wrapped presents spilling from beneath it. Then they rushed to the window to see if Old Jack had come with Santa to help deliver presents.

Maggie's hands and back ached, but the memory of the children's faces pressed against the front room window made her feel warm inside.

Grown now, the children had all moved off and had families of their own. Gregory was in Tulsa, Jonathan in New Orleans and Annette in Orlando. Each had moved as far away from the long Milwaukee winters as they could get.

Benji, she knew, was more to blame for the children moving away than winter. Maggie had chosen to take his abuse for thirty-six years but the children all had the better sense to get out and get far away from him when they were able.

She rubbed her hands together to warm her cold fingertips. She wondered if any of her children shared special family customs with their own children. She hardly heard from the boys anymore. Annette would call and check on her from time to time, but they were quick courtesy calls at best.

How nice it would be, she thought, packing more snow onto Old Jack, to have grandchildren to visit and awaken on Christmas morning to the lights and presents and a huge grinning snowman in the front lawn to greet them. It would be just like old times.

The sun would be up soon. Christmas would be alive with the delightful squeals of excited children and the pleasant rustling of paper as presents were torn open.

Sighing, Maggie trudged to the metal shed behind the house to retrieve a plastic storage box and the bag of coal she had collected the week earlier.

Boots crunching over snow, she watched her step with the help of the dim light pouring from the front porch. The snow seemed to glow in the murky dimness with the light reflecting off its surface.

There was no rush to finish before sunrise, but old habits were hard to overcome. She trod along, her feet sinking almost up to her knees in some places, until she made it to the shed. Unlatching the handle, she slid the metal shed door open. It made a hideous shriek, made even more hideous in the quiet, still morning. She hoped the screeching metal door had not disturbed any of the neighbors.

She rummaged around until she found the blue storage box. From within, she retrieved an old top hat and scarf.

Thirty-six years of marriage and Benji had never once helped with Old Jack. He had never helped with anything to do with the holidays except his attempts to ruin them, she thought bitterly.

Easily, she could remember Christmas mornings when Benji would not yet be home when the children awoke. He would still be out with his drinking buddies, or in some other woman's bed. One Christmas morning he called from jail of all places.

Then there were the years when she found him passed out on the front porch, or still in his truck, slumped over the seat, liquor spilled all over him. It was nothing to get a call from one of the neighbors informing her that he was passed out in their yard, sleeping restlessly in a nativity scene or among decorations.

One year, cursing and carrying on because dinner was not yet ready when he arrived home early, Benji raged until the children were frightened and crying. Becoming more angered when Maggie was unable to quiet the terrified children, he slapped her across the face, pushed her into the Christmas tree and left the house damning them all to hell.

No, Maggie never blamed the children for moving away or cutting their ties with their parents. She envied them. They were much stronger than she had ever been and for that she thanked God.

But even after they were gone, Maggie still decorated the house every year. She still put up a tree and wrapped empty boxes to put under it, and sent out Christmas cards and always snuck outside a couple of hours before dawn to bring Old Jack to life.

The top hat sat crooked on Old Jack's head. Maggie fastened the scarf around the snowman's wide neck. With the coal she fashioned Old Jack a lopsided grin, a nose and two eyes.

"Not bad," she mumbled with a smile. She began packing more snow around Old Jack's bottom and midsection. She had made him extra fat this year.

Benji had come home late the night before in a mood. Mean and surly, he had yelled and cursed Maggie from one room to the next. Fists waving in the air as he screamed, he pulled decorations off the walls, smashed them on the floor, spat on the tree and yanked the wreath from the front door. He yelled and hollered how Maggie was a stupid cow, how she wasted her time on decorating the house when nobody cared and how he had wasted his life with her. He damned her, wished her dead.

Thirty-six years of abuse had finally taken its toll and Maggie Anderson struck out, slapping her husband across his foul, vile mouth.

Stunned, Benji had just stared at her a moment. The look on his face said he could not believe the stupid cow finally reacted. Then, his rage boiling over, he grabbed her by the throat and pummeled her face with a tight fist.

When he was finished beating her, Maggie dropped to the floor choking. The room rocked out of control under her and she gasped to catch her breath. She cradled her face while Benji yelled at her and stalked off to the kitchen.

She feared she would be sick. Her face was hot and her left eye was swelling shut. She wished to die. Her head was full of his angry, screaming voice. He was yelling at her to come into the kitchen. She knew if she did not come into the kitchen, he would be back, beating and screaming and hitting even more fiercely.

Steadying herself on an end table, fighting a wave of nausea and dizziness, Maggie's fingers brushed against the base of the porcelain Christmas angel the children gave her as a gift one year when they were still little. Golden winged, the angel looked down at Maggie with sorrowful eyes as Benji continued to shout at her from the kitchen.

Beer in one hand, Benji was bent over in the refrigerator cursing when Maggie shuffled slowly into the kitchen. She was afraid to speak.

"I swear to Christ, Maggie, I kill myself to earn a paycheck and there's not one damn thing to eat in this house!" He slammed the refrigerator door shut and turned to face her.

Before he could utter one more curse, one more hate-filled obscenity, the porcelain Christmas angel crashed down upon his skull. It struck again and again, and continued striking, pulverizing flesh and bone, until Benji Anderson's head lay open on the kitchen floor and the angel's wings were dripping a dark crimson and the house was blessedly quiet.

Finished, Maggie stepped back to admire her handiwork.

"A little fatter than most years, but you look pretty darn good, Old Jack."

The sun was rising and Maggie could imagine the first of the children waking up on this glorious Christmas morning.

In a couple of hours she would call the children, her babies, to wish them all a Merry Christmas. She would tell them how much she loved them and missed them, and let them know it was safe to come back home if they ever wanted to visit. She felt in her heart this was going to be the best Christmas ever.

None of the children will believe me when I tell them their father helped with Old Jack this year, she thought as she returned the plastic storage box to the metal shed.

She smiled. Although her face was still swollen and sore, the smile felt good.

The nice thing about the Milwaukee winter, Maggie thought, was that no one would find Benji's body until at least April or May.

That would be when the spring thaw came, and Benji Anderson would come rolling out of Old Jack's fat, melting belly.

Still Life

The bitter taste of blood will forever be burned onto the creature's tongue, its brownish pigment forever stained across the creature's lips.

It survived on flesh, raw morsels of human flesh that sated its infernal hunger.

Blood drinker.

Flesh eater.

Abomination.

On twisted, grotesquely malformed appendages, the creature dragged itself across the dirt floor. Chains rattling, it crawled over the bloated body of a partially devoured woman. Gone was the life from the woman's eyes, but alive was her body with the feasting swarms of mealworms and bottle flies, hard-shelled beetles and other parasites of the dead.

It lurched to the far wall. Its every movement was an orchestra of exquisite agony.

A sluice of rainwater spilled down the stone and mortar wall. Greedily, the creature licked at the trickling wetness.

Too weak to return to the dark corner from where it had ventured, the creature rested. Cool and welcoming was the stone wall against its crooked, deformed spine.

All was quiet above. There was no moving about, no heavy footfalls.

In the quiet darkness, in the damp stink of rot and death and waste, the memories came to the creature. Phantoms from a different lifetime, they flooded the creature's mind like the spewing pus bursting from an infected wound.

* * *

The morning sun felt warm on Michael Cranston's face. With the winter months behind them, and the spring holiday quickly approaching, Michael noticed a renewed vigor on the campus as he walked from the faculty parking lot to the Science building.

Professor Cranston greeted several students and fellow instructors on his way to the office he shared with Professors Bloom and Davies. He had time enough for one cup of coffee before the day's first class. It was a ritual he fully endorsed, a process of jump-starting his brain before facing his early morning pupils.

Some time after twelve, during his lunch break, the phone in the little office rang. Michael had been blankly staring out the office window, watching students trod back and forth across the soccer field, vying for control of the checkered ball, as he ate a chicken salad sandwich.

It was Julianne, his wife.

"I have the most wonderful news," Julianne said enthusiastically, her words bubbling over with excitement.

"Do tell, darling," Michael replied around another bite of his sandwich. "I could use some wonderful news right now."

"Bad day?" Julianne asked, concerned.

"My students are restless and my lessons cannot compete with their plans for the spring holiday. Regardless of how ill prepared I feel most of them are for the examinations before the spring holiday, they are rambunctious and unwilling to pay attention to ready themselves." Michael was frustrated and overworked.

"Well, maybe this will cheer you up," Julianne started. "Geoffrey called this morning to say he was in town."

At the mention of his childhood friend, Michael's spirits did liven.

"When did he arrive?"

"Evidently he has been in town for nearly two weeks and just got around to calling us today."

"A typical Geoffrey stunt," Michael said with a smile.

"I invited him to dinner tonight."

"Splendid." Michael looked at his watch. It was twelve seventeen. "I could stop and pick up a couple bottles of wine on the way home," he offered.

"You read my mind." Michael could hear the smile in Julianne's voice.

"Love you," Michael said.

"Me too."

With that Michael replaced the phone onto its cradle, finished his sandwich, and prepared for his fourth period session.

* * *

Michael allowed his mind to wander on the drive home. On the way he stopped at the Spirits Shoppe and picked up the wine.

Thoughts of papers to be graded and examinations to be given and various students who were barely treading the academic waters slowly melted away and soon Michael was simply looking forward to spending the evening with his wife and friend.

Having become close friends while attending Thurston Academy, a private institute in Boston for grades tenth through twelfth, Michael Cranston and Geoffrey Boles shared a bond known only to the closest of brothers.

Upon graduation, Michael decided to further his education while Geoffrey optioned to conquer the world with both his love for adventure and the high-speed camera his parents had given him as a graduation present. Neither ever looked back.

For years Michael marveled over Geoffrey's extraordinary career in photography. He followed Geoffrey's many adventures in the pages of the most prestigious of news periodicals.

Geoffrey had a wonderful talent for capturing a specific moment of time in the camera's eye. Whether it be the gnashing jaws of a great white shark off the coast of South America, or the shell-shocked victims of political warfare, or the deadly beauty of an erupting Hawaiian volcano, Geoffrey's still-lifes breathed, lived and were forever immortalized in their sliver of time.

He had been best man at Michael and Julianne's wedding, and Michael cherished any time he could spend with his friend.

* * *

Geoffrey was fascinating Julianne with a tale about an Amazonian tribe he lived with for eight months to record their rituals in a photo journal when Michael arrived home.

Julianne greeted her husband with a loving hug and kiss. From Geoffrey it was a strong, solid handshake that quickly became a brotherly embrace.

"My God, you look good," Geoffrey said while Michael put the wine in the refrigerator to chill before dinner.

"How long are you back?" Michael asked, sitting at the kitchen table and inviting Geoffrey to do the same as Julianne put the finishing touches on dinner.

"I'm between assignments right now," Geoffrey said with a smile. "I thought a couple of weeks of rest and relaxation might be good for my weary soul."

* * *

After dinner they retired to the screened-in porch for more wine and more of Geoffrey's adventure stories.

Geoffrey began the specifics of his most recent assignment to Haiti when Julianne retreated inside to quickly refresh their drinks.

Michael listened with rapt attention as Geoffrey told of Haitian beliefs and superstitions, as well as his participation in an actual voodoo resurrection.

"It was my good fortune to be allowed to sit in on the ritual and capture it all on film. The supposed *bokor*, a self-proclaimed evil witch doctor of sorts, restored to life a chap who had been clinically deceased for six days." Geoffrey sipped his wine. "Of course, the man who was the object in the resurrection had never actually died. He had simply entered a trance-like state after being slipped a mixture of herbs and roots that froze his vital signs down to being virtually undetectable."

Again Julianne refilled their wineglasses.

"The resurrection ceremony itself was little more than Las Vegas-style theatrics. Candle lit, it was the mood the *bokor* created through his ceremonial garb and fevered chanting, as well as a handful of gunpowder thrown into the fire at the proper moment." Geoffrey laughed. Sipping more wine, he smiled wryly. "At the prescribed moment in the ceremony, the *bokor* slammed his fists upon the 'dead' man's chest. The shock of the repeated blows actually jump-started the fellow's heart and snapped him out of the trance. The poor chap all but jumped from his skin when he came 'alive,' gasping for breath and clutching at the Heavens. You would have truly believed he had really been brought back from death."

"Another?" It was Julianne's voice and it broke Michael from the reverie in which Geoffrey's tale had enveloped him.

"Sure, why not?" Geoffrey said, grinning like a schoolboy. "How about it, old man, one more?"

"Actually, I think I have had quite enough." Michael was suddenly aware of how light-headed he felt, of how numb his body was becoming.

"Nonsense," Geoffrey exclaimed, turning to Julianne. "Fill them to the brim, love. Tonight we are celebrating."

When Julianne returned with the drinks, Michael was flushed and sweaty. He was suddenly hot in the night's cool breeze. Julianne obliged him by turning on the porch's overhead fan.

"The effects of good food, good wine, and good company." Geoffrey raised his wineglass. "To us."

Attempting a strained smile, Michael raised his glass and promptly dropped it. The glass shattered across the stained plank floorboards.

"Sorry...I..." The words were choked from Michael's throat.

"You do look a bit peaked, old man," Geoffrey offered, sipping his wine.

Michael tried to stand, but his legs were weak and rubbery. The porch was spinning out from under him and the night sounds of chirping and buzzing and rustling intensified to a dangerous treble that threatened to burst his eardrums and leave him deaf.

Losing his balance Michael pitched forward. Smacking his head first on the top of the table, then again on the surface of the wood floor, he was swallowed into a warm darkness.

* * *

Slowly the world came back into focus for Michael Cranston.

His head throbbed where he had hit it. He attempted to reach for his head to rub it, but his hands did not move. They lay still on either side of him, lifeless and limp. He sat on the couch in the living room.

"I imagine all this seems a bit strange to you, old friend." Geoffrey stood before Michael wearing nothing more than the bathrobe Julianne had given him two years earlier for his thirty-ninth birthday.

"I wish there was something I could tell you to make all this right, Michael." Geoffrey walked out of his limited line of sight. Michael heard Geoffrey rustling in the leather backpack he carried with him everywhere. When Geoffrey returned, he had his camera. He took a picture of Michael on the couch.

"You're unable to blink," Geoffrey said in a fascinated tone, then snapped another. Then closer to Michael's face, the lens whirling into focus, he snapped another.

"Your eyes barely dilate," Geoffrey observed, taking another photo. Finally he set the camera down and sat on the coffee table facing Michael.

"I've loved Julianne since the first time I laid eyes on her, Michael. She has felt the same for me. I've wanted her for my own since I first made love to her, just hours before the two of you were married." He smiled sheepishly.

Michael was enraged. He wanted to scream out, jump up from the couch and throttle Geoffrey Boles until his fingers ached and the last gasp of breath was squeezed free of Geoffrey's lungs.

But his body would not move. It could not move. He was trapped. No sounds he could make, Michael was barely able to suck air into his petrified lungs.

Julianne was there then, her naked body glistening with sweat. Geoffrey stood and faced her. Julianne pushed Michael's bathrobe from Geoffrey's broad shoulders. Their lips met with a burning passion Julianne had never shared with her own husband. Kneeling to the floor they joined together and rutted in a fervor Michael had never experienced with Julianne. He watched as she allowed Geoffrey to explore places on her body that Michael had only ever known as forbidden.

* * *

Michael Cranston was a prisoner in his own body. His mind was sharp and clear, but the mechanics of movement had been lost. He was unable to roll his eyes or blink or even shed a tear.

But he was alive. The pain in his head and the pain in his heart were reminders. Only the living felt pain.

He cursed himself for never suspecting the infidelity of his wife. He watched until she and Geoffrey finally collapsed onto each other, their sexual hunger momentarily satisfied.

* * *

Eventually, after listening to the blast of the shower from the bathroom in the master bedroom, Michael saw Geoffrey and Julianne enter the living room.

They moved about quickly, regarding Michael as little more than a stick of furniture.

There were no sideway glances from Julianne, no apologies or attempts to make excuses.

Then Michael was hoisted into the air and laid over Geoffrey's broad shoulder. He was carried through his house and into the garage and shoved into the trunk of his own car. Then the darkness of the trunk swallowed him completely.

* * *

After a bumpy ride up Steeple Hill, a drive Michael knew well as he traveled it twice daily, five times a week, going back and forth to the university when classes were in session, the car stopped and the trunk opened onto the night.

He was lifted from the trunk and positioned behind the car's steering wheel. He noticed Geoffrey's Jeep parked on the road's shoulder next to his car, as he was moved from the trunk.

His head was yanked back and fingers were suddenly inside his mouth, prying his jaws open. Then came the familiar hot splash of bourbon. When it seemed he might choke, Geoffrey chopped at his throat to force the liquor down. His head was then righted.

Geoffrey splashed the bourbon about the inside of the car, and then dropped the bottle onto the passenger seat.

The car's engine roared to life.

No final words were spoken, or last minute reconsiderations made.

The next sensation for Michael Cranston was that of flying. That momentary feeling of weightlessness was finally interrupted by a horrendous crash and tumble as the car dove end over end down to the bottom of Steeple Hill.

When the chaos of the world around him finally settled, Michael's body lay still across the inside roof. After rolling out of control the car came to a rest bottom side up. His nerve endings cried out in a symphony of immense pain. It felt as if a rib bone had been broken off and used to stir his insides into a thick chum, then set aflame.

The shallow breaths his lungs still allowed sent a stinging pain throughout his body. He felt parts of his body shattered and torn open, weeping blood, but was unable to move to mend them.

He wondered if he would bleed to death, if maybe death would come and take him from such pain. But he reasoned that his heart was probably not pumping fast enough for him to be completely drained of life.

Surely, he thought, someone had heard the noise of the crash. Possibly the headlights were on and some traveler on the road above would see them and call for help.

All Michael could do was wait.

* * *

By morning, the inside of the car was crawling with curious creatures. Mostly insects, a squirrel had entered through the shattered windshield just before sunup and taken a couple nips of flesh from Michael's body, probably to save for later to enjoy with a hearty meal of nuts.

A line of ants marched across Michael's face, across his left eye and into his hairline where a cut laid open, still leaking blood.

With all his might Michael strained to make his muscles work. Even if he could move, he thought, all he would be able to mange would be to crawl through the shattered windshield and drag his broken body along on legs that felt totally useless.

Their faces, the coupling of their bodies, of Julianne and Geoffrey, had haunted him throughout the night. He half expected to see them outside the car. Maybe they were, but he was unable to see them. Maybe they had come back to make sure he was really dead, and not just zombified from a potion procured from a Haitian witch doctor.

If they were out there, watching him, Michael half expected them to get close enough to poke him with a stick. See how he would react. See if he would move if they took the pointed end of a sapling branch and dug it into one of his eyes until it popped free.

In his mind Michael cursed them over and again. He kept his mind so busy cursing them that he did not realize that he had been found, and that his salvation was at hand.

* * *

During the melee of the rescue, Michael became confused in all the faces that were peering in at him. Policemen, firemen, paramedics, rescue squad; there were so many different people in so many different uniforms looking down on him.

When a crew with reciprocating saws arrived, Michael felt the hot sting of sparks raining down upon his face as he was cut free and pulled from the wreckage.

The coroner pronounced him dead at the scene, but not before Julianne, sobbing, identified Michael as her husband.

In the thundering commotion around him, Michael could only hear bits and pieces of what Julianne was telling the near-by police officers, but he heard all the important parts.

"He's been so despondent about work... had been drinking heavily...was making no sense...so angry, so violent...left out like a madman...speeding off...was so scared...don't feel well...Oh, God...can't believe...can't...no...God, no..."

It was a good act, Michael thought, as his body was lifted up and laid to rest again. A young paramedic looked down at him and made an uneasy face. The paramedic reacted to something said to him with a vigorous shake of his head. Michael then felt the paramedic's gentle fingertips upon his eyelids, closing them, leaving him in darkness.

The sharp zip of the body bag as it enveloped him was the only sound in Michael Cranston's world.

* * *

There was no emergency to get Michael Cranston to the hospital. There was never any urgency for the dead.

Michael's mind blazed, questioning over and over if this was not truly what death was. Was it not possible for a body to still feel pain after it had died? Was it not a possibility that neither Heaven nor Hell existed, that there were no bright lights or flaming pits to welcome newly entered souls? Who knew for sure?

The ride was a short one, maybe twenty minutes into town, and Michael soon felt himself being pushed on wheels and slammed through double doors down a hospital corridor.

He heard the ring of an elevator bell, then felt the sensation of going down. He was pushed farther, and then came to a stop.

He heard the squeak of rubber-soled shoes on linoleum as people moved around him.

"Got a good one for you here, Pete." The voice was young, possibly belonging to the young paramedic who had mercifully shut his eyes earlier.

The body bag zipped open.

"A real mess, huh, Pete?" It was the young man again. "Guy got liquored up then took a nosedive down Steeple Hill last night. A broken bag of bones, huh? Had ants all over his face and in his eyes and mouth and inside his head when we found him. What do you think, Pete?"

If Pete thought anything, Michael did not hear the man voice it. All he heard was a heavy sigh, then Pete, an older man, asked the younger man to help move Michael's body out of the rubber bag and onto another table.

"A lot of dead weight, huh, Pete?"

"Do we know who this unfortunate gentleman is?" Pete asked in a tired voice.

"Yeah. He's a professor up at the college. His wife identified him at the accident site. A hell of a nice looking lady, too, Pete. Long blonde hair, legs that didn't stop, nice round..."

The younger man was interrupted when Pete requested the accompanying paperwork. Papers were signed on their proper lines and torn at their perforated edges and placed on a desk until they could be properly filled out and filed at a later time.

"Take care, Pete." Michael listened to the footsteps as they moved away from him. Double doors were pushed open and quietly swung shut behind the footsteps.

"Annoying little ass," Pete grumbled. Michael heard instruments being moved around atop a metal tray.

Michael felt a soft fingertip on his right eye and then the lid was opened.

Pete was a man possibly in his late fifties or early sixties. Gray hair and gray mustache, he looked tired.

When Pete opened Michael's left eyelid he stopped, his head tilted slightly in a curious manner.

"What's this?"

This is it, Michael thought. This is when they realize I am really alive. Barely, body broken, but still I am alive. My heart is still pumping, blood still flowing.

Surely, he thought hopefully, there was some kind of medicine they could treat him with to counteract the effect of the homemade zombie potion Julianne and Geoffrey had feed him, something to snap him out of the horrific paralysis with which his body had been afflicted.

Whatever Pete thought he had seen he simply shrugged off and gently closed Michael's eyes.

"Tell you what, friend," he began genially. "It's been a busy day and I've got to tend to old Mrs. Martling ahead of you. Poor dear was found hanging in her coat closet with a goodbye note pinned to her sweater. I've got some anxious relatives who want to see her put to rest quickly, and an insurance company who wants me to find out if the old girl was taking her anti-depressants like she had been prescribed. I'm going to let you rest the night, and then get to you first thing in the morning."

With that a thin sheet was pulled over Michael's body and he was shut up into the cold darkness of a refrigerated morgue chamber.

* * *

Michael awoke with a gasp. He sat upright in bed. His body was covered in sweat.

The lamp on the nightstand on Julianne's side of the bed flickered to life. Julianne was beside him, comforting him.

Gasping breaths, sucking in air, Michael slowly began calming down. He ran fingers through his sweaty hair.

"Whatever it was, it was just a nightmare," Julianne said soothingly. Her gentle fingertips glided down Michael's bare back.

"It was so real," Michael whispered as he caught his breath. His heart was racing, his head bursting with pain. He felt Julianne's lips on his neck. Her warm breath chased away the puckering goose flesh that was trailing down his spine.

He turned to Julianne. He felt embarrassed for the horrible thoughts of her that had played across his sleeping mind. He offered a wounded smile.

"Too much wine, I guess." Michael rubbed his temples. "And Geoffrey's horror stories didn't help much either."

Julianne smiled. The corners of her lips curved up into a grotesque smile as the ends rose up much too high on her cheeks. Then the flicker of a forked tongue played atop her lower lip before sliding back into the darkness of her mouth.

"It was no nightmare, old man."

Geoffrey was there, standing behind Julianne, his hands on her bare shoulders, smiling.

Michael's bathrobe, carelessly draped over Geoffrey's body, did little to conceal Geoffrey's nakedness. His stiffness poked from the bathrobe's folds and it too seemed to be smiling.

There was a sudden flash of light and then another. Geoffrey's right eye was now a dark, whirling camera lens, and his left an exploding flash bulb.

"You can't even blink, can you old man?"

Each time the lens whirled into focus, and the flash bulb burst into a blinding blossom of light, time seemed to stop. It ceased to exist momentarily in the presence of the camera's eye.

Again it flashed, then again.

* * *

The door of the refrigerated chamber opened on silent hinges.

Although Michael's eyelids did not flutter open, or his mouth form an early morning yawn, he was conscious of being fully awake.

Big hands pulled him off the cold metal slab. His body was dropped to the floor while the slab was slid back into the chamber and the door properly sealed.

Michael felt his body hoisted up and thrown across a massive shoulder, much bigger than Geoffrey's shoulder when he had been carried to the garage. He could see nothing, and his savior spoke in only low, inaudible grunts and mumbles.

He heard heavy footsteps echoing down the empty corridor. Next came the sensation of going up, in the elevator, and then he was hurried forward until he felt the cool blast of the night wind upon his skin.

The big hands slung Michael to the ground. The thin cover in which he had been sheathed inside the refrigerated chamber blew away in the wind.

A door squeaked open on rusty hinges. Not a car door, but more like the door on the back of a van or utility truck.

Again he was grabbed and hoisted by the big hands. Nothing made sense as he felt his body being shoved inside the truck. Something was humming. It sounded like a motor, like the hum of a refrigerator motor. It sounded just like the cold chambers back in the morgue.

Another door was opened, this one a sliding door that wheezed open on its track.

Michael was pushed and crammed and forced inside. When his left leg refused to comply with the demands of his savior, the big hands snapped the leg against its knee.

The door quickly slid shut, followed by the outer door slamming shut on its rusty hinges.

Nothing existed except for the explosion of pain that thundered throughout Michael's body. It was quite a while before he took notice of the vehicle's movement, or the frigidness of his new home.

* * *

The pain in his shattered knee never seemed to subside. The darkness wove a freezing cocoon around his body that numbed him to the bone and helped dull the pain, but the pain never completely went away.

Without knowing how many hours had passed since his abduction from the morgue, Michael eventually focused on the routine movement of the vehicle he was being held within.

It moved slowly, and in circles, and made numerous stops on its strange route.

Later, he noticed the music. Above the din of the cold box's compressor, he finally recognized the calliope music that immediately brought to mind the state fairs he had frequented with his parents in his youth.

When the vehicle stopped, the inside boomed with thunderous footfalls. The excited, bird-like chirping of children's voices always preceded the stopping of the vehicle, and the booming footfalls.

A door, just above Michael's head, slid open regularly and the big hands would grope in the cold darkness. At times, the big hands would brush against his cold flesh, or poke him, or pinch him, with the sounds of all the excited children so close.

Never once did he hear the driver utter anything resembling a word, not one understandable, recognizable syllable.

The slow circling continued, until Michael noticed a longer drive at a faster clip. They seemed to be traveling with more urgency now. There was no music, no stopping.

Eventually came the sound of brakes compressing, of tires crunching on gravel and of the outer door opening on its weatherworn hinges.

The compartment in which Michael lay stuffed opened quickly and the big hands grabbed him and pulled him from the frigid box.

* * *

He attempted to shut out most of the roughness, tried to ignore all the poking and pinching. The sound of packing tape being pulled from its spool made Michael think of a screeching bird of prey swooping down.

One of the giant fingers pressed onto Michael's left eye, threatening to pop the orb from its socket by brute force alone. The eye was opened and affixed with a piece of packing tape. Then the other eye was opened and secured.

Michael was unable to find words to describe the being that shared the mirror's reflection with him. It was a grotesque parody of the human form. Surely not a man, it was a beast, a nightmare thing made flesh and foisted into the living world.

The beast's body was unclothed, obese but muscular, powerful. The huge body was covered in a heavy down of fur-like hair. The bristling fibers covered the massive chest and back, and up and down the arms and legs. Everywhere there was hair, except for the head, which was bald.

Like tree trunks, the arms ended in huge hands with fingers like over-stuffed sausages. There was no neck, just the bald head that sat between the great expanse of the beast's broad shoulders.

Sloped lower on the cheek than the right eye, the beast's left eye appeared to be dead and non-functioning. The teeth in the hole of its mouth were broken and chipped, and rooted into gums black with decay.

Michael shuddered inwardly at the thought that this beast regularly interacted with children.

Still, nothing resembling a word emitted from the beast's mouth. Only the grunts and child-like murmurs, and little snorts of air through its ugly pug nose.

He wished he could look away from the reflection of the beast, to stand and run screaming from it, but his paralysis kept him captive in this living nightmare.

The beast had its beauty.

A dark wig of straight black hair flowed over Michael's shoulders. Various hues of make-up were smeared across his face in exaggerated swirls. His lips were red well beyond their outline. The eye shadow crept well beyond his eyebrows.

His body had been dressed in a floral patterned summer dress. Snapped back, his left leg now dangled broken over the edge of the chair in which he sat. His feet had been crammed into high-heeled shoes several sizes too small.

Michael's mind was wild, as if on fire. He continued to believe that as each new horror presented itself, his mind would eventually shut down and close out the atrocities. But his mind was sharp and seemed to focus more clearly with each new indignity.

The beast took Michael into its powerful arms. Its lips slathered over Michael's face. The fetid breath emitting from the stinking hole of its mouth covered Michael like thick oil.

He was laid gently onto the bed and rolled over onto his stomach. He felt the beast's tongue sliding over the backs of his legs.

The giant fingers pushed the summer dress up over Michael's thighs. Every fiber in his being wanted to cry out, bellow, and push away from the beast and run, run far, and escape the twisted, demented nightmare landscape unto which he had been unwittingly deserted.

His sluggish heartbeat began to thump faster, the clutch of fear squeezing it tighter. Michael was flush, hot with fear and he felt the first dribbling of sweat bubbling up from his pores.

The beast's big hands pushed Michael's legs open. They groped and touched and probed, then pulled Michael's body toward it.

At the moment of hot, searing pain, Michael's heart began beating wildly, the fear so thick as to be choking, a blasting gasp of air burst from his lungs.

His body lunged forward, toward the bed's headboard. All his joints and muscles were snapping, twitching, his entire body convulsing. He lay like a fish out of water, eyes wide and mouth gaping for air.

On its feet the beast stumbled away from Michael and nearly fell backward in its haste. It had been momentarily frightened and squealed a high-pitched shriek of despair, like a pig being butchered.

Michael did well to roll onto his back and command his body to sit upright. His mouth attempted to form words but his tongue was too thick yet for speech. He hoped the beast, the vile defiler of dead human beings, would, in some primal way, recognize his pleas for help.

His hands made weak fists, and every pain in his body was now alive, but now he had hope. Hope of discovery. Hope of rescue. Hope.

Suddenly, and before Michael could react to what was happening, the beast was upon him. Squealing and shrieking, the beast brought its heavy fists down upon Michael in a thunderstorm of stinging blows and pounding pain. Over and again, smashing Michael's face and chest, shattering the fragile bones just beneath the flesh. Dragged to the floor, the beast continued to pummel him with one massive blow after another. His face and chest were stomped upon, his neck and spine assaulted by the beast's heavy footfalls. Bones were splintered, flesh was torn and blood was spilled.

* * *

Michael lay in the warm pool of blood that drained from his demolished body. His brain still refused to cut off his suffering.

He heard the beast mumbling, grunting, and wondered how it had registered the strange event of Michael's awakening in its mind.

Satisfied that Michael would no longer refuse it, the beast dragged him back to the bed to sate its lustful cravings.

Afterward, the beast held him, cuddled him close and shed tears from its one good eye. Michael was unable to understand fully the tears, but he believed they were shed as the beast basked in the afterglow of birth. It had just taken part in a rebirth of sorts, a rebirth made of its own hands. It had just helped give life to a dead thing.

It held Michael close, crushing his smashed face into the thick brush of hair on its chest.

In the beast's arms, Michael Cranston silently prayed for death.

* * *

Early the following morning Michael was taken to the basement of the beast's domain. He was left on the cold dirt floor.

Legs useless, arms useless, unable to squeeze any sound from his crushed throat, Michael lay still. When he did try to move, his efforts were rewarded by an excruciating wave of pain that rocketed throughout his body.

Little slivers of light shone through the boarded-up basement windows. At one time Michael would have simply been able to stand before a window, pry free the boards from their rusty nails, break through the dirty glass panes and scurry through to freedom. But from where his body lay, the window seemed a million miles away.

The whole world was living and breathing just on the other side of the boarded up window glass, and he could do nothing.

In the cold darkness Michael wept. And it hurt.

* * *

Returning later that evening, the beast entered the basement with a thick leather strap and a length of chain.

After fixing the strap like a collar around Michael's neck, and securing it to the chain with a padlock, the beast did the same to the other end with another padlock and an eyebolt protruding from the basement's stonewall.

Finished, the beast poured out a helping of dried dog food onto the dirt floor.

Painfully, Michael moved his body toward the morsels of food. Unable to grab the food and put it to his mouth, he worked to eat the food from floor with his tongue.

Delighted, the beast cooed, like a small child watching a brightly colored balloon take flight into a clear summer sky, and clapped its giant hands excitedly.

* * *

Days had passed, possibly a week, when Michael heard the beast above fly into a whirlwind fury. Screeching and barking, stomping about and bringing destruction to all it touched, Michael hoped the ceiling above might come crashing down upon him, killing both himself and the beast.

Instinctively he knew the cause of the uproar. It only made a certain demented logic within the nightmare tapestry in which he currently existed.

The beast had tried to bring back another. Again it had tried to restore life to a dead thing, and met with failure.

Michael soon heard the heavy footfalls of the beast stomp down the basement stairs.

The door was kicked open and the beast stood momentarily outlined in dim light. In its arms was the body of a dead woman.

With a snort the beast dropped the body next to where Michael lay curled. After a moment it turned and left the basement, slamming the door shut behind it.

* * *

Michael sat in the cold darkness with the dead woman for several long nights.

When he became lonely or scared, he crawled into the dead woman's arms for comfort.

* * *

Eventually, he ceased to feed on the dried dog food the beast provided him. He hoped that in his broken physical condition starvation would soon propel him into death's awaiting embrace.

* * *

The beast brought another body to its lair and again it failed to create life.

Down in the basement the beast dumped the body of a young man next to the moldering, bloated body of the dead woman.

On its way to leave the basement, the beast stopped, noticing for the first time how high the pile of dried dog food was stacked. It turned and looked at Michael, then back at the pile of food.

The beast retrieved a folding knife from its back pants pocket then squatted at the body of the young man. Laying the blade to the naked skin of the young man's chest, the beast carved free a jag of flesh. It took the wet, flayed strip and offered it to Michael.

When Michael refused, the beast snorted and offered it a second time. Turning his head away, Michael whimpered like a hurt animal.

Rolling the flesh into a neat wrap, the beast grabbed Michael by the hair, jerked his head back, and forced the plug of flesh into his mouth. Michael spat it to the ground, choking.

The beast flayed another strip of flesh and shoved it into Michael's mouth. This time the beast covered his mouth with a huge hand and forced him to swallow.

Michael's stomach immediately rejected the flesh. He gagged violently.

Angered, the beast plucked the flesh from the ground and stuffed it into its own mouth. It chewed, then, like a mother bird feeding her young, it again forced Michael's mouth open and spat the chewed flesh into his mouth and forced him to swallow.

The chewed flesh oozed down the back of his throat like a giant, slow moving slug. It was rejected a second time.

Retching, Michael felt a giant blow slam into the side of his skull. His head was snapped back unmercifully against the collar and chain. Again a fist blasted upon him, then another.

The beast resumed feeding him after the beating until Michael's stomach learned to accept the new nourishment.

By the time the beast left the basement, all the flesh of the young man's upper body was gone, and there was a good-sized cavity in the body's midsection.

Michael hurt, but his stomach was bloated, full from the feeding.

* * *

Julianne and Geoffrey. The two adulterers returned from so long ago.

It pained Michael to continue to recall them. But in the quiet, cold darkness, theirs were the only visages his mind was ever able to conjure.

Sometimes he heard their whisperings, their lovemaking.

Sometimes he even believed they lay in the dirt before him on the basement floor. He would tear into their bodies with great vigor, ripping and chewing and drinking, consuming them and swallowing them, making them pay for what they had done to him.

For what he had become.

* * *

At times, the dank air was alive with the recital of prayer, the prayer for death. Other times he was completely convinced that he had already perished, and that he resided in hell.

Then there were the times when Michael Cranston was unfailingly certain that he would never die.

* * *

When it felt strong enough to return to its corner, the creature made slow, deliberate movements.

In the familiarity of its corner, the creature slept. It suffered fevered nightmares of mealworms and hard-shelled beetles nesting, and then bursting from its pulsating, screaming mind.

Only the heavy footfalls outside the basement door chased the grotesque nightmares away.

Another body was dropped to the dirt floor.

Fingers played over the nude form. Again the features were familiar to the creature.

It was she again, the woman who haunted the creature's memories.

Even in the darkness, the creature could see her face ever so clearly, hear her voice and smell her sweet scent.

Blood drinker.
Flesh eater.
Abomination.
The creature began to feed.

Visit to Grandma's

The children were overwhelmed with excitement. "Are we there yet? Are we almost to Grandma's?" they sang in unison, their little bodies bouncing in the backseat.

"Almost," their father said with a smile. He watched the children in the rearview mirror, winking at them. Noel giggled.

"I hope Grandma has a surprise for us," Christian beamed. The boy's blond curls were springy and some fell across his forehead into his blue eyes.

"I'm sure Grandma will have a treat for you," Mother assured. "She always does." Her smile radiated upon the twins.

"Just a couple more miles to go," Father announced. In unison the children clapped and bounced more vigorously in the seat.

When Grandma's farmhouse could be seen in the approaching distance, Noel squealed delightedly, "Grandma's!"

Wilson Barrows pulled into the driveway and drove up to the grand old house in which he had been raised. Christian and Noel had heard all the wonderful stories about their father growing up in the big house, out in the spacious country, away from the hustle and bustle of the city.

Christian and Noel were opening their doors before the car had come to a complete stop.

"Be careful," their mother warned sternly, watching them.

Running to the front porch they heard the big oak door creak open, saw their grandmother standing behind the wooden screen door.

"Grandma," Christian said, pulling the screen door wider so he and his twin sister could run into their grandmother's awaiting arms.

The old woman was as delighted as the children for the visit.

"My children, my little angels," the old woman beamed, hugging the children close. She was soft and warm and smelled of Sunday dinner and fresh baked cookies. "Come in, come in."

The screen door snapped shut on its spring. The crack it made when it slammed into the doorframe sounded like the report of a hunting rifle.

Wilson smiled and opened the car door for his wife, Kylee. Taking her hand he led her toward the house his father built. The clean country air tasted fresh and he breathed its richness deep into his lungs. Walking onto the porch Wilson opened the screen door for his wife, still the gentleman his mother raised.

The twins were chattering rambunctiously, each trying to win their grandmother's full attention, when their parents entered the kitchen.

"Do you have anything for us?" Christian asked excitedly.

"A surprise," Noel chirped. Her eyes were wide with anticipation.

"Children, stop it," Kylee said in a low, stern tone. "You know Grandma is not feeling well."

"A surprise," Grandma said, her smile as bright as the early morning sun. "Oh, yes. Yes, yes, yes. A wonderful surprise for two wonderful grandchildren."

Hopping on either side of the old women, the children followed their grandmother to the opposite side of the kitchen, to the door leading down to the basement.

"Be careful, little angels," the old woman said softly with the children behind her. She turned on a light that illuminated the dark, descending stairwell.

The wooden planks of the stairs creaked with the sudden weight upon them, sounding like painful moans.

"A surprise for the children," she repeated. She stepped off the bottom stair, followed the dark wall to the light switch. The children followed closely behind.

Their glee was expressed in their silent expressions of delight when the basement light revealed Grandma's surprise.

"Mom," Wilson sighed good-naturedly when he saw the surprise his mother had for the twins. "This is too much."

"Nonsense. These two angels are my only grandchildren. I'm entitled to spoil them, am I not?"

"I don't know that they've been good enough to deserve this," Kylee said with a sly glance at the children.

"Yes we have," Noel hurriedly blurted. The eight-year-old looked up at her mother with big, sad eyes.

"If Grandma says you've been good," Kylee said with a glance at her husband who just shrugged his shoulders, "I guess it is okay."

"I say it is okay." The old woman hugged her grandchildren again. "Go get your toys if you want to play a little while before dinner."

Christian rushed to a metal utility shelf against the basement's block wall, next to the washer and dryer. He returned with his grandfather's old toolbox. When it was new, the toolbox had been shiny and red but now it was dull, scratched and rusted in places. It thumped heavily on the floor where the boy dropped it. He and his sister fumbled with the snap latches and threw the lid open.

Little hands grabbed at the tools nestled in the belly of the toolbox. Most had been the tools their grandfather used when he was alive and working. He worked in construction all his life and continued to tinker well after retiring. There was a utility knife with a hook blade, a shingling hammer and various screwdrivers, clamps, pliers, snips and wrenches. There were other tools too, tools that belonged to the twins, tools they had found in their stockings on Christmas morning or had been given as birthday gifts. There was a black handled corkscrew, a long pair of sewing scissors, a hole-punch for working with leather, a battery operated carving knife and an electric charcoal lighter.

Each child had a favorite tool and grabbed it. Christian went to find Grandpa's orange extension cord.

Grandma smiled lovingly at her grandchildren. Wilson and Kylee held hands and watched.

"Can we take the tape off?" Noel asked. The little girl's eyes were round and innocent.

"I don't know if that's such a good idea," Kylee started, looking at her husband for support. Wilson said, "You know Grandma might not want to listen…" His daughter interrupted him before he could finish.

"Please, please, please," Noel begged. Her voice was cracking with anticipation.

"Of course you can," Grandma answered with a warm, glowing smile. Kylee gave her husband a sour look at their decision being overridden. Wilson gave her hand a gentle squeeze. Kylee knew there was no point in arguing with her mother-in-law.

Reaching out, Noel took the corner of the gray duct tape and ripped it away quickly. It was smeared with blood and stuck momentarily to her delicate fingers.

"What do you want from me?" the terror-stricken girl shackled to the basement's center support post screamed wildly.

An older girl, Noel guessed she was probably a teenager, no doubt still in high school. The girl's naked body was bruised and bloodied, covered in lacerations that still dribbled blood.

Dried blood was caked around her wrists where the shackles had cut into her skin when she struggled against the restraints. The bottoms of her feet were black with dirt and grime from the basement floor.

"You people are crazy!" she spat.

Noel stabbed at the girl with the corkscrew. The sharp point caught just underneath the girl's left breast and cut a jagged line, drawing more blood.

"Stop it," screamed the girl hysterically, struggling to move away. Noel followed her around the post and laid a hot searing line of pain down her naked back. The teenage girl screamed then broke down into sobbing pleas for mercy.

The little girl giggled. Her brother giggled behind her.

"I guess I'll get the overnight bags," Wilson said. He kissed his wife, then his mother, and then headed up the stairs. "You kids play nice. I don't want to hear any fighting," he added before he was gone.

The teenage girl continued to scream as Noel applied pressure on the corkscrew, which was poking her stomach. When the tip of the corkscrew punctured her flat belly, Noel gave it a vicious twist that made the girl wail painfully.

Grandma laughed, clapping her hands softly.

This was how Daddy met their Mom, Noel thought as she jerked the corkscrew free. Grandma had brought Mommy to the basement. She stabbed the corkscrew into the girl's shoulder.

"Grandma's tired," Kylee announced over the tortured screams of the girl. "I'm going to take her upstairs so we can sit and talk."

Noel smiled up at Grandma.

Mom helped Grandma up the stairs. Grandma seemed sick sometimes, but Noel knew she was still strong.

"My little angels." The old woman blew kisses to her grandchildren.

"Please stop," the teenage girl pleaded, sobbing over and over. Her eyes were wide with fear and pain and wet from crying.

"We'll stop," Christian started, stepping next to his sister. The heating coil of the electric charcoal starter glowed brightly in the dim light of the basement. It looked like a neon loop of orange heat.

"When we're done playing."

Pickford's Well

"I never been the superstitious type. I don't go in for ghosts or goblins. I never believed in UFOs, Bigfoot, the Loch Ness Monster or little green men."

There was a short pause on the tape.

"But there's something damn strange about that well on the Pickford farm."

Veronica Adams reached over and adjusted the volume on the recorder. Hank Zimmerman's voice boomed in the car.

"I'll never forget it. We were just a bunch of stupid kids. It was me and Jimmy Thompson, Eddie Wilks and Roger Franks." The speaker paused, clearing his throat.

"We were hanging around the old Pickford farm, just goofing off, wasting the day. The old man disappeared two years before and the whole place was grown over, a mess."

Fumbling to drive and read the handwritten map, Veronica steered the car onto a dirt road while the recorded voice continued speaking.

"It was summer. Eddie had a bottle of wine he'd taken from his grandfather. We were just grab-assing, getting drunk. We'd gone through the house, but it was cleaned out. Pickford's kids sold everything the old man ever owned. Sold everything but the property itself. Old man Pickford was never much of a farmer. Truth be told, his little plug of land was never much of a farm."

Following the road, Veronica passed an ancient looking cemetery then drove up a slight incline overrun with tree limbs reaching across the road from either side.

"He never could get anything to grow on the property," Hank continued. "His crops always died. It always seemed like maybe something was bad wrong with the land, like the soil was rotten. Who knows?"

The road was bumpy and Veronica cursed each time the undercarriage of the car scraped the rocky path.

"Anyway, it was getting on dark and we were all feeling pretty good. The wine had us high and the lazy summer sun drooped in the sky and there wasn't anywhere in the whole wide world any of us had to be." There was a pause while Hank took a swig of beer.

"The day was pretty much finished and we were all getting hungry. We decided it was time to head back into town, find some burgers, and then drive around a couple hours, whatever. We were heading to Eddie's car when we heard it, the moaning. It was sort of like when the wind blows and kind of howls, but it sounded more like someone who was hurt, in pain."

In the distance, Veronica spotted the driveway leading up to the Pickford farm.

"So we started looking around. It was dark and Jimmy started pitching a fit, said that it sounded like someone familiar, that it was someone we knew. We all figured he'd just had too much to drink, but he kept carrying on, getting more and more freaked out. His eyes were bugging out of his head and this moaning was on the wind, it was all around us.

"We tried to convince ourselves it was only an owl, something that couldn't hurt us. But the longer we listened, the more it really did start to sound like someone we knew."

Veronica navigated the car up the drive.

"We looked all around and finally Jimmy found the well out in the backyard. It had a round piece of plywood over its top, and the moaning was coming from inside the well. Jimmy pushed the cover off and the moans just echoed out the well's mouth, like bubbles rushing to the top of a soda bottle."

There was a moment of silence on the tape.

"Eddie said we needed to go back, needed to get the police. Jimmy was bent over the well, hanging over and reaching inside. He was hollering he could see somebody at the bottom and that it was somebody we knew.

"Roger was on one side of Jimmy holding on to him and I was on the other. Roger couldn't see anything in the well and ran to the car with Eddie. Eddie started honking the horn and I'm tugging like crazy on Jimmy's arm, trying to get him to come with me, and he just pulled away."

More silence.

"I looked in there but I didn't see a damn thing."

Hank paused again, coughed.

"I told Jimmy I was going with Eddie and Roger. I told him we'd be back with the police and the fire department.

"Jimmy didn't pay me any mind so I ran off to the car. When I got to the car I heard Jimmy screaming over and over again, 'No! No!' I looked back and he was reaching into the well.

"Eddie was honking the horn and Roger was yelling at me to hurry up. I got in the car and we sped into town."

More coughing filled the air on the tape.

"I never saw Jimmy Thompson again."

Silence.

"We came back with a couple deputies. When we couldn't find Jimmy, they called out the fire department and sent a man down into the well.

"All they found was the dried out bottom of the well. There was no Jimmy Thompson, nobody."

The voice of Hank Zimmerman fell silent and Veronica's voice emitted from the recorder's tiny speaker.

"That was Mr. Hank Zimmerman, age forty-seven, recounting his encounter with Pickford's well, August second, nineteen seventy-three. This interview was conducted on October sixteenth."

The car stopped in front of the dilapidated farmhouse. The old house looked somehow sinister, a little evil in the dwindling light of day.

When the snap of the recorder turning itself off startled her, Veronica laughed at herself.

"That's real good, Veronica," she mumbled as she collected her camera and put a fresh cassette in the recorder. "Letting the spooky stories spook you."

When she was out of the car, she snapped a number of photos of the old farmhouse. The waning sunlight helped give the structure an eerie glow.

It would make the perfect photo for the book cover, she thought as she clicked away.

Veronica had spent the last eighteen months on the road, traveling the southern states, collecting ghost stories for her new book *Modern Ghost Stories of the South*. She had sought the most obscure tales for the book, from the smallest buttonhole communities she could find.

In her travels she located the ghost of a man who regularly haunted a quaint little bed-and-breakfast in Tennessee. The man died at the inn, making love to his new wife on their wedding night. Naked as the day he died twenty years before, the man still roamed around the inn's rooms, searching for his beloved wife.

She recorded the creepy story told by a retired mill foreman in Mississippi of a worker who had his skull crushed in a piece of machinery, and who returned to haunt the third shift workers, always searching with outstretched arms for his mashed head.

In a backwater town in Georgia, Veronica spent seven nights on the property of what was once the Spencer Drive-in, waiting for the crumbling screen to come to life and show a couple minutes of some old movie. The locals claimed it was just Martin Wick, the deceased owner, still running reels from beyond the grave.

A dozen stories she had collected, twelve scary tales of true-life haunts and ghostly beings.

In Alabama, while investigating Elksboro High's spectral quarterback, Veronica first heard of the Pickford well.

A cashier at the supermarket where the quarterback had bagged groceries before his untimely death in a car accident told Veronica that if she wanted a real ghost story, the Pickford well was it. She told Veronica the well swallowed up at least twenty people that she knew of, if not more.

Seizing the opportunity to add another chapter to her book, chapter thirteen, Veronica quickly got on the road to Higginsville, home of the haunted well.

She snapped another photo of the farmhouse.

Arriving in the little town three days ago, Veronica had a tough time getting anyone to talk to her about the well.

On her story-collecting journeys, she found bored, chatty waitresses and old men sitting on benches outside barbershops and pharmacies to be some of her best friends. They were always willing to spill the beans on some local legend, especially if they thought it would get their name mentioned in a book.

It didn't take her long to realize she had no best friends in Higginsville. No one talked to her more than two seconds after she mentioned the Pickford well.

Finally, enough asking around and two crisp twenties at a beauty salon got a couple of questions answered.

For starters, the Pickford well had never been officially blamed for any of the missing people in town. According to Belle Sanders, the beautician, the well was searched so many times and nothing was ever found inside it, the police stopped searching it when someone new went missing.

"But," Belle elaborated, talking clearly into Veronica's tape recorder. "Folks around here have always suspected something suspicious about that old well. There've been too many weird things happen out there.

"Like old man Pickford suddenly disappearing like he did in '71. That never made sense. The man was seventy-nine years old. Where could he have gone? Then Jimmy Thompson went missing in '73. Two little girls went missing in '75 and a guy with the electric company was out there checking on some lines in '78 and no one ever saw him again either. In 1984 a real estate agent was up checking on the place and he was never seen again. All they found of him was his pick-up truck parked out front of the place and a pen with his name on it at the base of the well.

"Each time the rescue workers went into that well, they never came out with anything more than a bunch more questions."

Belle began talking in a hushed tone; as if afraid one of her clients might overhear what she was saying.

"I heard they tried to fill it with concrete one time. That's unofficial, of course. They supposedly took three big trucks up there and filled it to the top, but it didn't work. In a couple of days all the dried concrete was gone, like the well had never been filled. People still went missing."

Belle rattled off more incidents, speaking clearly into the recorder's mike.

Veronica felt a tingling behind her ears as Belle talked away. It was the tingling she got when she heard a great story.

The Pickford well was the big one, the story that would sell the whole book.

'The Well That Ate People,' was the chapter title which came immediately to her mind. She had envisioned a cover illustration showing a well with a skeletal hand reaching out over its edge. Maybe, she thought, they could draw bloodied teeth all around the well and really exploit the story.

Looping the camera strap over her head and around her neck, Veronica slowly approached the old farmhouse.

She pressed the red record button on the little tape player.

"If houses can take on life and feel the world around them, the Pickford farmhouse looks as if it has led a brooding life of pain and agony. With its askew shutters and weather-torn siding, the Pickford house is not a place where evil dwells. It is the place where evil was first given life."

Smiling, she flipped the recorder off. It was that kind of sizzle which helped to sell the steak.

Of the people Veronica had spoken to, only Hank Zimmerman was willing to talk about his experience at the Pickford well.

She had found him on a stool, spilled over a bar top in a dingy little tavern. Reluctant to talk at first, a couple drinks greased his jaw and got him talking until he could not stop.

The other boys mentioned in Hank's retelling of the night Jimmy Thompson disappeared had long moved away from Higginsville and the well that consumed their friend.

She pressed the record button again.

"Although Ellias Pickford's farmhouse still stands, it seems a strong enough wind could topple the structure, crumble it to its very foundation in an instant."

Carefully stepping over a patch of overgrown brush, Veronica stepped onto the front porch. The boards groaned like the reawakened dead beneath her weight.

As if expecting to see someone, she peered through a dirty window next to the door. She grabbed the door's handle and gave it a twist.

The door creaked open on rusty hinges.

Inside the farmhouse was a shambles, obviously the victim of vandals and vagrants, and the air permeating the house was sour. Veronica took a number of photos in various rooms while she still had a little sunlight left to use.

Satisfied she had enough photos to accompany the text, she clicked the little tape machine onto record.

"Gutted and abandoned, the Pickford house no longer holds even the memories of ever being a home. Gone is the family who once lived there. Gone are the children who once ran through its rooms and played. The holidays and happy times once celebrated within its walls are long forgotten. This is a dead place now."

Careful of each step, she made her way through the belly of the house. She moved into the kitchen and found a door leading out to the back yard.

From a broken window in the kitchen she saw the well. The plywood cover Hank Zimmerman had mentioned was gone. The well jutted from the ground like an odd, decrepit growth. Its mouth was a wide gaping hole of darkness.

Moving quickly to utilize the last of the dying sun, Veronica snapped a picture of the well framed within the broken windowpane. Then she pushed through the back door.

"A simple stone structure, the well sits less than fifty feet from the ramshackle farmhouse," she spoke into the recorder, and then swapped it again for the camera.

Using the last of the film on the roll, Veronica easily captured the eerie ambience enveloping the stone well.

"Could the eldritch moans from the Pickford well be those of the dead, voices from beyond the grave? Could the moaning Hank Zimmerman and his friends heard that night have been the frenzied gasps of trapped souls trying to communicate with the living? Where are all the unlucky people who have supposedly fallen into the well? Where could they possibly have gone? Only the victims of Pickford's well will ever know the answers to these questions."

A cool wind blew through the night and Veronica felt a chill run down her spine.

The idea of being so far out in the country, away even from small town civilization, was making her a little jumpy. Living, eating and breathing ghost stories for the past eighteen months was not helping either.

The property behind the farmhouse was barren and ugly. Veronica doubted it ever grew anything more than frustration and ill feelings.

Another wind blew, rustling the leaves in the surrounding trees, and on its tail end Veronica thought she heard the sound of someone moaning.

Goose flesh puckered the back of her neck.

"Hello?" she called out, knowing no one was there.

But somebody was there... and moaned again.

She was certain she heard it that time, knew beyond a shadow of a doubt that it was not the wind.

"Settle down, Veronica. Don't go and wet your pants just yet." She took a deep breath.

The memories of a pathetic drunk in a rinky-dink little bar had her nerves tied in knots and the sudden darkness was only helping to put her on edge.

She heard the moaning again. This time it sounded familiar.

"Mr. Zimmerman, is that you?"

Veronica stood between the farmhouse and the well and nothing moved. She was getting angry now, feeling like the butt of a joke for a drunk who had entertained her for an hour for a couple free drinks. Now he was having the last laugh.

"This is not funny, Mr. Zimmerman!"

Again the moan bellowed out, this time louder.

All of a sudden, like lightning, two flashes of light exploded, one after the other, from within the well.

Stomach twisted, Veronica felt sick. She was suddenly aware of a metallic clicking and realized she was shaking so badly she was hitting the tape machine against the camera.

Every urge screamed at her to leave this place, to run to the car and drive away. She no longer had any desire to write about this dead place or take any more pictures of it.

But she felt drawn, drawn to the well.

The blasts of lights she had seen. They were real. They had filled the inside of the well, if only for a few fleeting seconds.

Another moan echoed out of the mouth of the well. It filled her head.

Someone was really down there.

Without realizing it, Veronica had crept up to the well's stone edge. The yawning mouth was open wide before her. She peered into the dark abyss and saw nothing.

"Is someone down there?"

She listened as her voice echoed. Then all was silent.

"Can you hear me? Are you hurt?"

Her words were swallowed within the tunnel of nothingness.

Then the most painful wail she ever heard burst from the darkness of the stone well. Cold fear gripped her heart and squeezed tightly.

"Oh my God! Can you hear me?"

Moaning, mumbling noises flew out of the well like frightened bats from a cave.

"What?" Veronica called out. "I can't understand you."

Robert Freese

Muddled words, parts of words, echoed up from the darkness, strung together in a nonsensical gibberish.

"I can get the police. Are you hurt?"

Blackness swallowed her as she reached into the well and continued to call out.

"Can you see me? What is your name?"

A beam of moonlight momentarily filled the well and what it showed her sent a bolt of shock blasting through her.

It's not possible, her mind shrieked, trying to rationalize what she saw.

Losing her balance, she grabbed desperately for the well's edge. The stone surface was smooth and cool.

"No!" the voice bellowed out as Veronica pitched forward and tumbled into the black belly of the well.

* * *

Everything was dark, pitch black.

Veronica's head hurt horribly. A throbbing pain beat a steady rhythm throughout her body.

Sitting upright, she felt a lancing pain roar through her legs and up her side. Her left leg was bent grotesquely backwards. Wincing, she unfolded her broken leg from underneath her. Fresh pain blasted from the wound.

Veronica took in her surroundings.

She sat unmoving on the dry floor of Pickford's well.

Occasional beams of moonlight filled the well, reflecting off the smooth circular stone wall surrounding her.

The opening of the well did not look that far away, maybe only fifteen feet or so. She thought she might be able to climb up the wall, using the jutting stones as hand and foot holds. She moved to pick herself up.

When she put weight on her broken leg, she fell over with a moan of pain that echoed out into the night.

Tears in her eyes, holding her crumpled leg, Veronica's heart skipped a beat when she heard somebody just outside the well.

Was it possible Hank Zimmerman followed her out to the old farm to scare her for a laugh and his joke went horribly wrong? Had all his crazy talk put ideas in her head that made her see and hear things that weren't there and caused a horrendous accident? Now she was at the bottom of the empty well with a broken leg and the thought of Hank Zimmerman leaving her there had her terrified.

Trying to call out for help, she was unable to find her voice. The pain from her leg rocketed through her body and all she was able was a ghastly moan that echoed within the well.

Veronica was frantic to get Hank's attention. Maybe he didn't even know she had fallen into the well. Maybe he had simply followed her out to the farmhouse to make sure nothing happened to her. All the maybes fluttered around in her head like wasps from a stirred-up nest.

Suddenly, she realized the camera was still looped around her neck. The lens was cracked but the flash didn't seem damaged. She fired off two quick blasts of light before the flash stopped functioning.

That would be enough, she reasoned. Surely the light would have gotten his attention. There was little chance that if Hank Zimmerman was near the well, he would miss the flashes of light.

At the top of the well, the silhouette of a head peeked over the rim. It looked like a woman with long hair.

"Is someone down there?"

A bolt of terror slammed into Veronica like lightning.

How was this possible? Her mind screeched those four words over and over again unable to make sense of what was happening. Her breathing accelerated rapidly, as did her heartbeat. She felt it pounding in her chest, like a man buried alive, beating on the inside of his casket, trying to escape before the last breath of air left his coffin.

"Can you hear me? Are you hurt?"

The words filled her head. Fresh tears spilled from her eyes. She tried to call out but still she could not find her voice. She tried to stand, but her leg buckled beneath her and sent new pain exploding throughout every nerve ending in her body.

"Oh my God!" the familiar voice echoed down. "Can you hear me?"

Sobbing, cradling her destroyed leg, Veronica finally found her voice and screamed out, "Get away from the well! Get away!"

"What?" the voice called back. "I can't hear you."

"It's the well! Get away from the well!" She was desperate to make the woman understand.

"I can get the police. Are you hurt?"

The shadow figure of the woman reached farther into the darkness of the well.

"Can you see me? What's your name?" the voice from above called.

Then a beam of moonlight momentarily filled the well. It illuminated Veronica lying on the well's bottom.

Ashen-faced and full of shock, the woman lost her balance.

"No!" Veronica screamed as she watched herself tumble into the dark belly of the well.

* * *

Everything was dark, pitch black.

Veronica's head hurt horribly. A throbbing pain beat a steady rhythm throughout her body.

Sitting upright, she felt a lancing pain roar through her legs and up her side. Her left leg was bent grotesquely backwards. Wincing, she unfolded her broken leg from underneath her. Fresh pain blasted from the wound.

Veronica took in her surroundings.

She sat unmoving on the dry floor of Pickford's well.

Big Hairy's Last Stand

Richard Monk was more than a little irritated. In fact, the more he thought about it, he admitted to himself he was outraged. Outraged and deeply offended.

A combat veteran by age twenty-three, Monk had served four consecutive tours of Vietnam and was discharged with full honors. Returning to an America gone mad, where war heroes were spat upon, Monk hopped the first freighter out and spent the next seventeen years as a gun for hire. Mercenary, bounty hunter, hit man or smuggler, Monk took whatever job paid top dollar.

Now he was little more than a babysitter for the punk filling the Cadillac's passenger seat, Scott Riley.

Monk had been more than infuriated when Mr. Pierce insisted the rookie accompany Monk on the routine pick-up. He had gone on hundreds of such pick-ups by himself in his years of service to Mr. Pierce, and this time was no different than any of the others.

Mr. Pierce was a man who had been a good employer for the past dozen years. He explained it would do the kid well to learn from a pro, pick up a couple tricks of the trade as it were.

"The kid's wet behind the ears and you're the best person I've got to show him the ropes," Mr. Pierce said, bringing the whole discussion to a close.

It was bullshit, prettied up and perfumed to sound and smell like a compliment and Monk knew it.

Monk hated Riley from the moment he swung by the kid's apartment to pick him up.

Riley brimmed with smart-ass attitude. Monk sized him up as being nothing more than a TV cowboy, a little know-nothing punk who grew up watching too many shoot-'em-up action movies as a kid, always believing what the boob tube showed him.

Riley whined incessantly about the early morning assignment and how he hadn't had enough time to eat breakfast before Monk arrived. He was also unkempt and sloppy, wearing jeans and a jacket with a wrinkled tee-shirt underneath.

Monk hated sloppy. He hated unkempt and he hated anything even slightly resembling smart-ass. It was very easy for him to hate Scott Riley.

Riley was a bucketful of stupid questions from the time he got into the car. He first asked about some of the action an "old-timer" like Monk had seen, followed by his never-ending barrage of questions concerning the task at hand.

All the while Monk allowed his mind to wander to more pleasant things. Such as snapping the kid's neck like a chicken bone and tossing his body out onto the side of the interstate.

The kid's lip-dancing ceased for roughly twenty miles when he realized Monk was paying him no attention and then started anew about the absence of his morning meal.

The .357 in Monk's shoulder holster had been a gift from a wealthy Venezuelan exporter whose daughter Monk had rescued from kidnappers. He wanted nothing more than to pull it free and redecorate the kid's face with bullet holes.

Instead, Richard Monk kept driving in silence, paying attention only to the road in front of him.

* * *

The Cadillac was eating up gas faster than a Sumo wrestler with a tapeworm let loose on an all-you-can-eat sushi buffet.

Manny's Filling Station was a relic from the past; perched off the side of the interstate exit thirty miles outside of Indianapolis. Manny's sold gas and oil, with two pumps on a concrete island out front, and a dingy little garage behind the island that emitted the sounds of country music and the occasional whirl of a pneumatic tool.

There was no convenience store offering microwavable snacks, milk and bread, beer and condoms, dirty magazines or three dollar and ninety-nine cent cassette tapes of the Best of Hank Williams, Jr. or Waylon Jennings.

Manny's traded solely in gas and oil and Monk liked that. He was comfortable with that. It was simple, just the way he preferred his life. Monk strove to keep his world uncluttered, neat, orderly and above all else, simple.

"I'm going to see if they have a candy machine," Riley mumbled. He slammed the car door behind him.

"Easy," Monk snapped. He moved to the gas tank, opened it and then stuffed the nozzle inside and started filling the metal beast with high octane.

"What can I do you for?" It was a grungy-faced mechanic in grease-smeared coveralls opened enough to reveal an equally filthy tee-shirt that read, 'Hoosiers do it on the court.'

"You wouldn't happen to know how close we are to the Winchester Twin, would you, pal?" Monk set the nozzle to run on its own. He took a squeegee from a pail of dirty stinking water and went to work cleaning away the dried insect carnage that coated the windshield.

"The drive-in movie?" The little guy scratched his head.

"One and the same," Monk returned with an easy smile.

"Sure. It's just a piece up the road here." He nodded down the blacktop highway that stretched away from the interstate. "Twenty, twenty-five miles at best."

"Fantastic," Monk replied, returned the squeegee to its bucket of swamp water.

"You know," the mechanic started with a look of concern, as if he was attempting to figure an algebra equation in his head. "They don't open 'till tonight. You know, when it gets dark."

The pump clicked off, indicating the tank was full. Monk returned the nozzle, replaced the cap on the car's tank and retrieved his wallet.

"Guess I just want to find a good spot early." He handed the mechanic two twenties, waited for his change.

After paying, Monk got back into the car and fired up the engine. Riley returned, slinging his body into the passenger seat. Again he slammed the door behind him.

"You slam that goddamn door again I'll make sure your head's in it," Monk warned disgustedly.

"The damn snack machine was broken," Riley said. "The soda machine was broken too."

"Poor baby," Monk muttered. He pulled the Cadillac onto the highway and sped off.

* * *

The sky behind the giant Winchester Twin Drive-In Theater sign was quickly changing from a dark blue to an ugly purple. The sky looked bruised. Monk wanted to be back on the road before the impending storm erupted.

The marquee beneath the crossed Winchester rifles announced a dusk-to-dawn comedy cavalcade. None of the titles listed were familiar to Monk.

"I thought all these old drive-ins had been paved over and turned into shopping malls," Riley commented with a smirk.

Monk navigated the Cadillac past the huge marquee and up a gravel path to the ticket booth. There was a neon 'open' sign in the front of the booth's glass window that was waiting for night so it could glow its brilliant bars of color.

Inside the booth stood a blond man in sunglasses. Solidly built, the man looked like a granite statue with skin pulled over its rocky surface.

Monk stopped the car at the booth and rolled down his window. "We're here to see Mr. Sebastian. We represent Mr. Pierce."

The goon eyed a clipboard, one hand never wavering far from the butt of the .45 at his side. He looked up. "Mr. Sebastian is waiting for you in the snack bar."

With a nod, Monk drove the big car up the gravel path to the snack bar, which was painted like a log fort from some old western movie. They passed rows and rows of metal speakers perched like birds in wire nests on the sides of silver posts.

"Try to keep your mouth shut," Monk warned as they got out of the car and greeted another man who sat on a stool outside the snack bar. He stood up as they approached.

Goon number two was almost an exact replica of the goon in the ticket booth, only with a crew cut of brown hair. "Gentlemen." He held a battery operated metal detector in one hand.

Monk stepped forward with his arms raised.

The goon swiped the detector up one side of Monk's body then down the other. He tensed slightly when the detector found Monk's .357.

"Let's take it out nice and easy, Pop," the goon instructed, no change in his voice.

Monk removed his sidearm and placed it atop a wide-mouth trash receptacle painted like a hungry cowboy eager for a mouthful of garbage.

The goon turned to Riley.

"I'll save you the effort, potato-head." Riley smirked, retrieved his 9mm and placed it next to Monk's .357.

A creature of habit, the goon swiped Riley before he allowed either man entrance into the snack bar.

* * *

The snack bar was huge, cafeteria-like. The double-sided concession counter was flanked on either far wall by giant picture windows. Each window faced one of the Winchester's huge outdoor screens on either end of the lot. On a wall opposite the counter was a bank of pinball machines and video arcade games. The walls that weren't primarily made up of window glass were covered in vintage film posters. Some of the chrome-framed posters brought back long ago memories of when Monk used to cruise the passion pits of Chattanooga for a piece of Friday night tail.

"I don't 'spect y'all cousins are here for the show, now are ya?"

Monk turned toward the voice.

"Mr. Monk," the little round man said with a nod of greeting. "Mr. Riley."

"Mr. Sebastian." Monk returned the nod. He offered his hand, which the little man took and pumped vigorously.

Franklin Sebastian was as tall as he was wide. Red-faced with a dark curly beard that concealed any indication of a neck, his long wavy hair was pulled back into a ponytail. An impeccably neat white suit stretched across his girth. Accompanying Sebastian was a woman who stood at least six feet tall and whose beauty made both Monk and Riley catch their breath.

Her ebony skin was smooth and flawless. Her long, luxurious black hair was pulled back and fell down her sharp shoulders in a dark, silky cascade.

"Y'all cousins look parched," Sebastian drawled. He chewed his words as if they were a thick, spicy jambalya.

"Why don't you offer our visitors a cold drink, Ms. Tiffany," he said to the woman beside him, patted her backside to prod her into motion.

Robert Freese

"Mr. Monk, Mr. Riley, would either of you gentlemen care for a Royal Crown Cola, Crush or root beer?" Her voice was soft southern velvet and it felt wonderful in their ears.

"I'm fine, thank you," Monk answered.

"Root beer," Riley blurted. His eyes were securely fixed on Ms. Tiffany's supple curves, like a coyote clocking a hen house. "Any chance of getting something to eat? I'm starved and I haven't had a chance to eat today."

The muscles in Monk's face tightened as he tensed. He made tight fists and struggled not to kill the kid right there in front of Franklin Sebastian.

"This ain't no soup kitchen, hickory-nuts," Sebastian drawled irritably. "The cold drink was offered in hospitality. I should take offense, but I can tell by looking at you, you don't know no better."

Sebastian scrutinized Riley for a long, frozen minute. Monk thought the little fat man might give the order to his goons to have the kid gunned down and save Monk the effort.

"Forget the hospitality, whistle-dick. We need to get this transaction in gear. Y'all ain't the only two cousins I got business with before showtime tonight. Come on."

Monk and Riley followed Sebastian outside the snack bar and around the corner of the building to a door marked 'storage.'

"I don't suppose your Mr. Pierce informed y'all on the specifics of the drive up here, did he Mr. Monk?" Sebastian fumbled with a ring of keys.

"No sir. We were only given a map with directions and instructed to bring the big car," Monk answered. He did not care for the smile curling up on either side of the fat man's abundant cheeks.

"Yes, sir, Mr. Monk, the big car indeed." Finding the storage room key on the ring, Sebastian inserted it into the lock.

"Y'all cousins hold on to your peckers 'cause this here thing is gonna knock y'all's pee-pees in the dirt."

With a twist of the knob, Sebastian threw the door wide open.

* * *

Instinctively, Monk reached for the .357 but found only the empty holster.

The world tilted wildly. He felt tipsy, as if affected by a few shots of phantom whiskey. It was stuffy, humid all of a sudden. He found it was getting hard to breathe.

Monk felt completely swallowed up in the pitch black of the creature's eyes.

"What is it?" Riley asked first.

"That be Ms. Tiffany's baby sister, cousin," Sebastian roared with laughter. "How 'bout I set y'all up on a dream date?"

The creature lay in a ball on the storage room floor on a makeshift pallet of blankets and hay. Its arms were tied behind its back, it ankles shackled. A heavy chain connected to the collar around the beast's neck stretched to where it was secured around one of the storage room's metal support beams.

Although it was lying with its knees against its chest, Monk guessed the creature would be nearly seven feet tall when standing unencumbered.

Thick tangles of ropy hair covered its muscular body.

"Jesus." Monk's mind was having a difficult time accepting what his eyes were showing him.

"Believe it, cousins. That there is the real McCoy. Guar-ron-teed." Sebastian continued to smile widely.

"Big boy here is the legendary Bey-Bey Thai. The Fouke Swamp Monster. Sasquatch. Bigfoot. Whatever ya'll care to call him. We just been callin' him Big Hairy around here." Sebastian patted the creature's flank.

"You caught him?" Riley asked, eyes wide. He squatted for a better look.

"Hell, no, cousin. Do I look like a hunter to you? I got people in my employ that are capable of acquiring such things when someone like your Mr. Pierce calls."

"But this can't be real," Monk said, barely above a whisper. In all his experiences, he had never encountered such a fierce creature.

"Not real? You smell that funk in the air, cousin?" Sebastian inhaled deeply. "That's one hundred and ten percent Louisiana swamp monster. If you can't believe what you're seein' and smellin', come on over here and grab a handful. It ain't no costume, you can be sure, cousin." He patted the creature roughly, noticing Monk taking a step back.

"Now, don't you worry about Big Hairy here none. He's as docile as a kitten with bag of catnip. He's jacked to the stars on tranquilizers. He can't hardly fart let alone try and hurt a hair on your head."

As if on cue, the creature let out a pitiful groan. Its eyes rolled around, then settled back on Monk.

"I don't know why your Mr. Pierce would want such an ugly, foul stinking thing," Sebastian said and scratched the thicket of hair on his chin. "But it is exactly what the gentleman ordered."

"Jesus," Monk mumbled a second time for lack of anything else to say.

"Y'all cousins best pop them peepers back into your heads and close them gaping mouths. Y'all got a long drive ahead of you and it looks like a lot of it is gonna be in bad weather. I advise you to get Big Hairy on home 'fore he wakes up. He wakes up, he's gonna be hungry." A wild twinkle lit Franklin Sebastian's eyes. "And y'all cousins absolutely will not believe what Big Hairy here can chow down on when he wakes up hungry."

* * *

The sky was covered in dark splotches, filled with swollen storm clouds.

"It's almost five," Riley announced. It was the first either had spoken since leaving the Winchester Twin Drive-in.

Monk glanced noncommittally at his watch and grunted. His attention went back wholly to the road ahead.

"Christ, man, would it kill you to stop somewhere so we could get something to eat? You've got to be hungry too. You've been driving nonstop all day."

As much as Monk hated to admit it, the kid was right.

"I don't want to leave that thing in the car alone," Monk replied.

"We can go some place that has a drive-up window. We won't even have to get out of the car."

The kid had a good point.

* * *

The first spatters of rain began dotting the Cadillac's windshield when Monk pulled into the parking lot of Billy's BBQ Shack. Except for a red pick-up truck and the rusted out ghost of a '78 Buick Skylark Coupe, the lot was empty.

Billy's was the only eatery the exit offered. It sat surrounded by hilly woodlands and dense forest as far as the eye could see.

It had no drive-up window.

"Stay here," Monk said as he got out of the car.

"Hell, no," Riley replied hurriedly. The kid was out of the car and in the rain before Monk had his door shut. "That ugly son-of-a-bitch can stay out here by itself."

The kid looked genuinely scared and Monk didn't blame him. A chill had stayed with him since first peering into the beast's heavy-lidded drug-glazed black eyes. He did not like being in the car with the thing any more than the kid did. But he also didn't like the idea of leaving the creature alone, even for a few minutes.

Rather than argue, cuss or threaten, Monk headed toward Billy's BBQ Shack. Riley followed.

* * *

The inside of Billy's was warm and dry and lit mostly by the neon beer signs that hung on the walls. There was a big, tinted picture window that faced the parking lot, and from just about anywhere inside, Monk was able to keep an eye on the Caddy.

"Can I help you?"

The waitress materialized magically from behind the glass counter full of gums and candies, pecan log rolls and souvenir Billy's BBQ Shack tee-shirts.

Riley ordered and paid for a meal to go first, then Monk.

Monk took a seat at a table that afforded him the best view of the Cadillac. Riley took a seat at the same table opposite him. They were quiet while they waited for their food.

"What do you think that thing really is?" Riley asked finally. He was playing with a white sugar packet.

"I don't know," Monk responded solemnly, his gaze never leaving the big car out in the storm. "And I don't care. I just want to get the damn thing to Mr. Pierce and put an end to this miserable day."

* * *

The creature stirred in the belly of the big car's trunk. It inhaled the wonderful aromas that seeped into the darkness.

Slowly, like a lifting morning mist, the fog was clearing from the creature's mind. A notch of white-hot hunger gnawed painfully in its gut.

Its instincts told the creature it was time to eat. The hunger drove it. Nothing else existed in the world other than the hunger and the desire to sate it, the desire to feast until it could eat no more.

Easily, the bands around its wrists and ankles snapped free. The creature's oversized hands beat frantically on the metal womb that enveloped it, beat frantically for a way out of the darkness.

* * *

Two guys in hunting camos, one wearing a camouflage ball cap, sat together at a center table, and a lanky fellow in a cowboy hat sat by himself at a corner table and finished his plate of ribs.

Monk watched the waitress bring two more cold bottles of beer to the camo guys. She then moved to the front counter where the cowboy had sauntered up to pay for his meal.

A bell dinged in the window between the kitchen and the dining area.

"Your orders are ready," the waitress said while thanking the cowboy for eating at Billy's and stuffing his greenbacks into the till.

"Finally," Riley said and stood.

She placed the white bags full of food on the glass counter top and went to get their drinks.

Monk froze as he stood up.

It did not register at first, but now he was sure of what he was seeing. Outside, in the rain, the back end of the Cadillac was being beaten savagely from within.

"Shit!" He bolted for the door.

* * *

The cowboy had stopped in his tracks in the parking lot, half turned around, not sure where he should go next. The Caddy was hopping on its back end just a few feet away, giving the shocks a good working over.

"Get away from the car," Monk yelled. The weight of the .357 was in his hands.

The car stopped.

All was silent except for the constant pounding of the storm.

The cowboy was frozen where he stood, as if standing on a land mine.

Riley appeared in the parking lot next to Monk, the 9mm preceding him.

"Step away slowly," Monk instructed the cowboy. "Move over this way, towards us."

Before the cowboy could navigate two steps, the Cadillac's trunk lid blew off its hinges like the top of a volcanic pressure cooker exploding over.

Everything happened in a flash, a blur.

The cowboy never knew what hit him.

"Goddamn," Riley screamed over the din of the storm. He had the 9mm spitting fire and noise.

Most of the cowboy's face was stuffed in the creature's gnashing maw when its attention turned away from its downed prey and it raced toward the kid.

Riley kept firing and Monk felt the warm wash of blood splash him as the kid was instantly torn in half. It happened so fast, Monk had no chance to react.

Monk felt his simple, uncluttered world slipping away from him. His ears boomed with the slurping and chewing sounds of handful after handful of Scott Riley greedily being crammed into the creature's mouth.

Without firing a shot, Monk began moving back towards the restaurant. His movements were slow and deliberate. He did not want to attract the creature's attention.

Inside Billy's BBQ Shack he pushed the entrance door shut behind him.

"We need to barricade the door!"

The door between the kitchen and the dining area swung wide. A bald cook brandishing a double barrel shot gun stepped through.

"I don't know what the hell's going on out there but Darla's calling the police and I think…"

Concentrating more on talking than walking, the cook lost his balance and stumbled forward.

Shotgun thunder filled the inside of Billy's BBQ Shack when the cook fell to the tiled floor.

In a blossom of red, gray and white, the hunter in the camouflage ball cap's head disintegrated in the blast of buckshot.

Monk tasted the man's blood in his mouth, felt spongy flecks of the man's brain and flakes of the man's skull freckling his face.

Darla the waitress began screaming hysterically.

The cook picked himself up off the floor.

The lights flickered once, came back on and then flickered again but stayed off for good.

Thunder clapped outside. The window Monk used to keep an eye on the Cadillac outside suddenly exploded inward. Glass shards showered the inside of the restaurant.

The remaining hunter was grabbed and pulled through the shattered window.

Horrified, Monk leveled the .357.

They heard the man's tortured screams over the raging storm outside.

After a crack of lightning, the creature stepped through the remains of the picture window. In one hand it held the hunter's arm, torn off at the shoulder and still wearing its shirt sleeve. Hanging by the hair in the other hand was the hunter's head. An ugly pie slice of glass jutted from the hunter's left eye.

"Son-of-a-bitch!"

The bald cook had the shotgun cracked open. Frantically he fed it two fresh shells.

"Don't," Monk yelled. The gun in his own hands shook violently.

Dropping the hunter's head the creature swung the arm like a Louisville Slugger and went upside the cook's bald skull. The arm-club smashed off the side of the cook's head with a dull thud.

Disoriented, the cook dropped the shotgun, staggered and was grabbed up by the creature in a ferocious bear hug.

Darla was screaming wildly and Monk watched as bloody spit and froth spilled from the cook's gaping mouth. His head was a fiery red, the veins were blistering atop the freshly shaven pate.

When the thunderclap of the cook's snapping spinal column blasted the air, Monk winced and felt his stomach flop. The creature folded the big cook as if it were folding a fancy dinner napkin.

The burning taste of bile inflamed the back of Monk's throat.

Darla was nearby, crouched behind the front counter. The woman was weeping, mascara running down her face like wet paint. She was choking on her sobs.

There was a momentary explosion of shattering glass. A twister of glass shards and assorted gums and candies, pecan log rolls and tee-shirts whipped around the inside of the restaurant for a chaotic instant. The creature destroyed the glass counter with two massive blows.

Monk knew he had to move, had to react. He had to command his muscles to act, jump into motion. Two shots blasted from the .357. Amazingly, neither slug found their mark.

A shadow fell upon him. Monk felt as if he had been swallowed whole. The .357 fell from his shaking hands, uselessly spun on the bloodstained floor.

Time froze as the creature stared down at Richard Monk.

The creature's eyes were murky cauldrons of swirling blackness. Within them Monk recognized a primitive, yet incredibly determined, will to survive.

He stopped breathing when one of the creature's oversized hands grabbed him by the throat and picked him off the floor. His legs dangled uselessly as the creature's grip on his throat tightened.

Just when he thought he was going to pass out, Monk pulled from the last of his reserves and suddenly found himself striking at the creature's arm. He pounded the beast's forearm, which felt solid, like wood wrapped in thick sheet metal.

With its free hand, the creature grabbed Monk's swinging fists, held them together and squeezed. Intense pain rocketed throughout Monk's body as the vise grip squeezed harder, set every nerve ending in his body aflame. Bone was ground up, pulverized in the creature's giant, powerful hand.

Hot tears ran down Monk's cheeks. His insides felt hot and watery.

Without warning, the creature slammed him onto the wooden floor. The creature brought its heavy foot down on him, stomping on his spine. There was a loud crack and then all of the pain in Monk's body ceased to exist.

A sweet, warm darkness rushed over Richard Monk and swept him away.

* * *

It was still raining when he awoke. The rain was cold and stinging his face. He swayed from a tree, his arms secured over his head. He realized he was no longer covered in clothes. Except for the rain on his face, he felt nothing.

Monk saw Darla. She too was naked. The woman lay in a ball. She was clutching her stomach with one hand, the other between her legs. Tears rolled down her cheeks and she made tiny, pitiful sounds.

The creature appeared after some time. It dropped a pile of sticks then bent and grabbed Darla by the ankle.

The woman gave no fight. In fact, she did nothing whatsoever to push away from the beast or run away. She was dragged out of Monk's limited line of sight.

Monk swayed in the tree for a long time, the forest quiet except for the grunting of the creature.

* * *

Monk wondered how far into the hills the creature had taken them. It had moved them twice now. How far away from the interstate and civilization were they? He wondered if anyone could see the fire, or at least the smoke from it.

Darla sat by the fire, eyes wide but blank, seeing nothing. He doubted she even knew where she was or what was happening to her any more.

Monk had been amazed the first time he watched the creature build a fire. It was still amazing. He watched with rapt attention when the creature, Big Hairy as Franklin Sebastian had called him, rubbed two sticks together until fire was born.

In fact, Monk thought often, a lot of the things the creature did were amazing. Like how it cooked its food over the fire with spits made from tree branches.

How it refused to allow Darla to go hungry was amazing too. When it prepared food, the creature always made sure Darla ate, even when she refused. The creature would push hot morsels of meat into her mouth then force her to swallow.

Everything was so unreal. It was all like some kind of bad drug trip, or fever dream. Sometimes Monk was unable to tell the difference between being awake and being asleep.

He could no longer talk because of his crushed esophagus, but sometimes he made noises to get the creature's attention. The creature would just look at him with its head tilted to one side, like a curious dog regarding a rabbit in its back yard.

* * *

Monk felt nothing when the creature snapped his left leg off at the knee, just as it had done before to his right leg.

He was astonished with the creature's knowledge and skill in applying a tourniquet. Although its hands were far from gentle, the creature applied just the right amount of pressure to keep Monk from bleeding to death.

Having long abandoned any hope of being rescued, Monk thought more and more on how long the creature planned on keeping him alive.

He was fed a diet of berries and leaves and Darla was prodded to give him water from a nearby stream. His body was always kept dangling from the tree, his arms secured over his head.

Over and over Monk wondered if the creature would continue devouring his lower half, eating its way up, or if it would eventually untie him and begin feasting on his arms.

On occasion, he would force gibberish from his mouth, like a baby, and try and hold conversations with the creature. He cursed the beast Big Hairy, demanded to be let free; taunted the beast to finish him, kill him. But he never received any kind of a response other than a cursory glance from the creature.

No answer.

No smart-ass comment.

Nothing.

Surely, Monk thought, hoped, prayed; death would come to him before he was little more than a torso and head lying on the cold forest floor.

Monk watched Darla sit by the fire. She always held her dirty, cut-up knees to her chest. She always seemed to be shivering, always crying.

The creature was always nearby. As of late it had begun sharpening a flat rock it found in the stream, fashioning it into a sort of crude axe head.

A cool breeze whispered through the trees.

Richard Monk swayed gently with the breeze.

Demon Con

Ryan Scott moved with the flow of bodies congesting the dealer's room. A makeshift highway had been created by the tables running on either side of the walkway full of people.

There was too much to see, Ryan thought as he stopped briefly at a table displaying and selling model kits of famous movie monsters from the '50s. On display were the robot from *The Day the Earth Stood Still*, the brain creatures from *Fiend Without A Face* and the upside down ice cream cone alien from *It Conquered the World*.

Marveling at the smallest details of the assembled model kits, Ryan was amazed that someone had the patience to put the kits together and make them look so great. He had little skill when it came to assembling models and even less when it came to painting and detailing them. But Eddie would definitely want to check the table of models out if he hadn't already.

Looking up, Ryan scanned the giant room for his friend but had no luck locating him. He could be anywhere, lost in the crowd of moving people, or in the autograph room, standing in line to get his posters and stills signed.

Eddie would show up soon enough. He always did.

People in costumes milled about with older fans attending with small children. Ryan was always surprised at the mix of people who attended the horror conventions, everyone from little kids to grandparents.

Those not in costume wore tee-shirts of their favorite horror and science fiction film heroes. Ryan saw people in old school *Star Trek* and Dr. Spock tees as well as shirts featuring Mike Nelson and the 'bots from *Mystery Science Theater 3000*. Horror shirts were emblazoned with blood-soaked images of the Cenobites from the *Hellraiser* series, Leatherface from *The Texas Chainsaw Massacre* and silk-screened one-sheet posters for such 42 Street grindhouse event films as *Ilsa: She Wolf of the S.S.* and *Mark of the Devil*.

Of all the places he had ever been, Ryan always felt at ease among the like-minded people who attended the horror and sci-fi cons. He moved from one table to the next, checking out the wares each dealer offered.

After spending some time poring through boxes of three-dollar film posters then talking to a dealer who sold collectable toys, Ryan came to an oversized table stacked with boxes full of old books. A placard standing in the center of the table read, "The Mystic Bookshelf."

"How's it going?" Ryan asked the dealer sitting behind the table.

Bespectacled with curly red hair and a bushy moustache, the dealer seemed preoccupied and did not acknowledge Ryan's greeting.

So be it, he decided, giving it no importance. He began looking through the titles the dealer offered. Most were older volumes, first editions that were so out of Ryan's price range he felt uncomfortable touching them.

One title that caught his eye was *The Outsider and Others*, a collection of H.P. Lovecraft short stories. Hardbound, it looked quite ancient, much like the tomes Lovecraft wrote about in his stories. It was wrapped in plastic with a green price sticker on the upper left hand corner of the book.

He nearly choked when he saw the book's selling price.

"Five hundred and fifty dollars," he said aloud, unable to keep it inside.

Ryan's intrusion on his thoughts snapped the dealer from his daydream. He seemed to suddenly notice Ryan standing before him and offered a crooked smile.

"I'm sorry?" The dealer pushed his spectacles up the bridge of his nose.

"Is this price correct?" Ryan held the book up so the dealer could see the price on the cover. "Five hundred and fifty dollars?"

"Oh, yes," the dealer said quickly, reaching out and gently taking the book. "Yes, it is." He held the book a moment before continuing.

"This was the first ever published collection of Lovecraft stories. August Derleth edited the volume and put it out under his Arkham House imprint." He seemed to struggle a moment, as if the book were sapping energy from him. "1939, I believe. *The Outsider and Others.*" His crooked smile returned. "Five hundred and fifty dollars. It is a deal, as it is stained with water marks but still very readable. It should have been up with these other books. I get so forgetful sometimes." Without waiting for Ryan to respond or make an offer, the dealer turned and set the book on a rack behind him with other costly tomes.

When the book dealer turned back around he asked, "Was there something I could help you find?"

This guy is a creep. Ryan kept the thought to himself. "I'm always on the lookout for any Robert Bloch books I don't have."

"Bloch," the dealer repeated quietly as he scanned over his volumes to see what he could locate. "A shame it is that most people do not realize Mr. Bloch wrote more than the novel *Psycho.* A true master of the macabre he was." He found a box with several Bloch titles.

Looking over the books, Ryan found a number of editions he did not have. He began the process of deciding which he could afford to splurge on. Each of the books was priced much higher than their original seventy-five cent and dollar cover prices.

Picking out the three he had to have, Ryan continued scanning over the titles and found a Ray Bradbury short story collection he didn't have.

After checking his quickly-depleting funds, he paid for the four books.

The book dealer wrapped them in a plastic grocery bag and handed them to Ryan.

"Thanks a lot."

The dealer paid no attention to him as Ryan moved away from his table of books.

Ryan was quickly swallowed up in the never ending wave of people. He continued forward until he came to a table of videocassettes. The dealer behind the table was talking to a girl in a black dress and lots of black eye make-up and seemed not to notice Ryan walk up. He began scanning over the titles the dealer offered and became lost in the film titles.

"Hey man, you dig on Italian cannibal flicks?"

Ryan looked up from the rows of videotapes and watched the dealer pull out a red box from underneath his table. The girl he had been talking to was gone. The box was full of more bootleg videos. The titles of all the movies were inked in dripping, red lettering.

The dealer was gangly, with long black hair and a shag of beard covering most his face. Ryan thought he looked like an old hippie. While the bootlegger ran a finger down the spines of the tapes in the box, Ryan noticed that he wore black leather gloves.

"Check it out. *Cannibal Holocaust*. Widescreen, uncut, straight from the Japanese laser disc. This is the cleanest, most pristine print you'll find, dude."

Sure it is, Ryan thought. The pristine print was obscured throughout by Japanese subtitles, not to mention the optical blurring of nudity imposed by Japanese moral groups. Real pristine.

"If you know anything about Ruggero Deodato, you know *Cannibal Holocaust* is his masterpiece. All the gory goodies for ten bucks. All the tapes in the red box are ten bucks a piece or six for fifty."

"I'll take a look," Ryan said with little enthusiasm. The bootleg video scene had changed so radically since the advent of digital videodiscs that most bootleggers whose stock in trade was selling sixth generation video dubs of foreign released laser discs was nearly extinct. All of the other video bootleg dealers at the con were trading in copied DVDs. Ryan wondered how the dealer even made enough money to survive.

.

"What about the maestro, Lucio Fulci? I've got uncut, widescreen versions of both *The Beyond* and *The House By The Cemetery*. Beautiful copies, man."

"I've got them both on DVD," Ryan responded. "On Special Edition discs." His eyes were scanning over the titles, searching for a diamond in the rough, some obscure title that he had not collected on tape or which had yet to score a DVD incarnation.

The longer he looked, though, the more he realized it was a bust. The guy had nothing he needed. Most of the stuff he could simply download and get a better copy. He began to drift away from the bootlegger's table.

"Hey, wait a minute, man," the dealer pleaded. "I know you like Dario Argento, right? Check it out." He removed a tape from the box. *"Phenomena.* This is the director's cut, man, completely uncut and uncensored. It's twenty minutes longer than the American version. This is from a German video source, with subtitles."

Ryan could not believe the guy. It was like the dealer was fifteen years behind the times. Bootlegging foreign laser discs on to tape seemed so primitive.

"I've got it on DVD," he said with a smile. "Thanks though." He began to turn to go check out a horror magazine and comic book table when he felt a tug on his arm.

"Hey, man. I may have a little something you don't have on DVD." The dealer said "DVD" as if it tasted sour in his mouth.

Ryan watched as the dealer again went underneath his table. This time he retrieved a single videotape in a plain black slipcase.

"What do you know about Paolo Sacchetti?"

Paolo Sacchetti was an Italian director acclaimed for his series of violent horror films based on actual demon lore, and Ryan knew all about him. *Demon Death Day, Virgin Demon Lover, Demon Masque* and *Demon Resurrection* were all regarded as classics by aficionados of hard-core Italian gore films.

After a twelve-year absence from filmmaking, Sacchetti came out of his self-imposed retirement to film his new demon opus, *House of Demons*.

Unfortunately, Sacchetti and the one hundred and twenty-seven other passengers on his flight perished in a horrible air accident minutes after leaving Milan's International Airport. Rumor had it that Sacchetti had the only existing print of the movie with him on the plane.

He felt an excited tug in his stomach.

"*House Of Demons*," the dealer said with a smile, pleased to see Ryan was hooked.

"That movie's not even supposed to exist." Ryan felt his mouth going dry. "It was destroyed when Sacchetti's plane crashed."

"That's the rumor," the dealer said. "The way I understand it, no one in the Italian film industry trusts anyone else. The producer, Antonio Lentini, had a copy of the work print. You know, in case anything happened. As it turned out, something happened."

Ryan watched as the dealer shuffled the tape from one hand to the other.

"It's incomplete, and time coded. It's not got any of the sound effects or music and it's in Italian. But from what I understand you can follow it easy enough."

"You haven't watched it?"

"Who has time? I don't watch half this stuff." He swept a hand over his inventory.

Ryan was skeptical. This deal was beginning to smell like a rip-off.

"How did you get a copy?"

"You know, man, I don't even remember. I get stuff from all over, at shows, from other collectors. People send me stuff all the time in trade."

Ryan still wasn't sure if he was experiencing a moment of incredible luck or if he was about to be bent over. This could be one of those moments most collectors always dreamed about, but never truly believed would ever happen. Provided the dealer was on the level.

Ryan had Sacchetti's entire filmography on DVD, and the shock maestro's last film, his lost film, would be the crown jewel in his collection.

"I didn't know if I was gonna pull this out or not," the dealer began. "It's kind of creepy having it. You know, since the guy who made it just died. I was told he was on his way to America to try and find a distribution deal for it."

The dealer was suddenly sounding like he was not interested in selling the tape.

Robert Freese

"But I can see you're a fan, man. I only have this one copy though, and I hate to let loose of it before I make a copy of it, but I got to eat, you know? Those damn DVDs are putting me out of business."

"How much?" Ryan finally asked, retrieving his wallet. "Ten bucks like the others?"

"Ten bucks? Hell no, man. What part of the 'possibly the only tape of this movie in existence' story didn't you catch, bro?" The dealer held the tape in a tight grip. "Didn't you hear me when I said this was the only copy I had? This thing could be a gold mine, man."

Ryan had heard this spiel from countless dealers in the past, especially from bootleg video dealers. Once they realized they had something you wanted, it suddenly became the 'last one.'

"Twenty?" Ryan asked.

"A hundred dollars," the dealer responded quickly.

Ryan felt as if he had just been slapped in the face with a cold, wet hand. A hundred bucks for a rough copy of a film that had supposedly been destroyed sounded like a scam. The dealer probably figured Ryan wouldn't even know he'd been ripped-off until long after the convention was over. He could be handing the dealer a hundred bucks for a blank cassette for all he knew.

Because of such scams, Ryan and Eddie always brought along a VCR to hook up to the hotel's TV when they attended horror conventions.

"How do I know this is the real deal?" he asked.

"You'll just have to trust me, man."

"I've got a VCR up in my room. I'll be able to check it out in a few minutes."

"Even better." The dealer didn't flinch. Ryan had seen bootleggers balk at the mention of a nearby tape machine and drop the whole transaction.

He thought a moment longer. "It's worth fifty to me," he finally said.

"That's cool, man. I thought you were the dude it was worth a hundred to. Sorry for wasting your time." The dealer went to return the tape to its place under the table.

"Wait a sec," Ryan said. "How about seventy-five?"

"A hundred, man. I got bills, you know? Hauling all this stuff from con to con costs money. Hell, man, I'm losing some major bread selling it for a hundred but I'm desperate here."

Sure, Ryan thought, but hating himself because he knew the dealer had finally broken him down.

"All right, I'll take it. That's why I come to these things." He pulled three twenties, a ten and two fives from his wallet.

"Me too, man. Me too." The dealer smiled and exchanged the videotape for the cash.

When the dealer handed Ryan the tape he felt the slightest shock from the exchange, like static electricity. He could not believe he had the lost Sacchetti film in his possession.

* * *

"Wha-ja find?"

Ryan jumped. It was just Eddie, but his friend had sneaked up behind him and slapped him on the back.

"God, Eddie, you scared the hell out of me."

"You know, it's Halloween. I guess everyone's entitled to one good scare." It was Eddie's best impression of the sheriff from *Halloween* when he bumped into the Jamie Lee Curtis character and startled her. Ryan just shook his head. He had known Eddie Peoples since grade school. They made a strange duo; Eddie was the athlete of the two, well built and muscular, while Ryan was the brain. More than once Eddie had kept

Ryan from being picked on in school and in exchange, Ryan had helped Eddie pass his more difficult classes. But their mutual interest in horror movies and monsters had formed a bond of friendship that had lasted into their early twenties.

"So what's the tape?" Eddie was wearing a black tee-shirt that had dripping blood-red words which read, '*Vampire Chicks Suck and Swallow.*'

"I don't know yet." Ryan put the videocassette into the grocery bag with the books he just purchased and then noticed the girl next to Eddie. She was attractive, slim, about twenty and wearing a black tee adorned with the ghostly white image of the graveyard ghoul from *Night of the Living Dead*. On the back of the shirt, in bold green lettering were the words "*They Won't Stay Dead!*"

"This is Kristi," Eddie said, introducing the dark-haired girl. "We met in line to get Michael Overton's autograph. She's a huge *Dead Things* freak too."

"Hi," she said with a pretty smile. She had a black plastic art tube on a strap slung over her shoulder. The art tubes were popular among convention goers to help carry and protect rolled movie posters.

"You missed it, Ryan. After we got Overton to sign our posters I got over to the Screamies table to meet Annette Cage. Kristi's taking my picture with her and Annette hikes those huge boobs of hers up onto my arm. When I look down I can see right down her shirt and trust me pal, those buddies weren't corralled in any wonder-bra. I assure you."

"Eddie!" Kristi playfully punched Eddie in the arm.

Ryan smiled. His friend had always enjoyed ogling the scantily clad scream queens and femme fatales.

"Are Brinke Stevens and Debbie Rochon still over there?" Ryan asked.

"Oh, yeah. Wait till you see what Debbie's wearing." Eddie made an exaggerated gesture like his eyes were popping out of his head. Kristi playfully punched him again.

"Cool. I've got a *Witchouse III* poster I wanted both of them to sign."

"So what did you find?" Eddie nodded toward the video-tape in his friend's hand.

"Oh," Ryan said with a shrug of his shoulders. "Just something that sounded too good to be true." He instinctively gripped the bag tighter, afraid of losing the video.

"You didn't get hosed on another rotten dub did you?"

"I don't know. I think I'm going to run up to the room real quick and check it out."

"Cool." Eddie looked at his watch. "Meet us in thirty minutes outside the screening room. Jack Dubose is previewing his new flick *Vampire Dawn*. After the preview he's only going to be at the autograph table signing stuff for an hour."

Ryan looked at his own watch. "Will do."

"See you there." Eddie took Kristi's hand and guided her back into the throng of people.

Ryan left the dealer's room and followed the hallway to the hotel's main lobby. There, he caught an elevator up to the fifteenth floor and then found the room he was sharing with Eddie.

* * *

The room was freezing cold.

Ryan and Eddie had been attending horror conventions all over the country for years, and every time they got to their hotel room, the first thing Eddie did was turn the room's air conditioner down as low as it would go. It was just one of his quirks.

Ryan slung a bag full of stills, folded movie posters, lobby card sets and signed 8x10s onto his bed. He noticed that Eddie had been up to the room at some point; his bed was littered with monster model kits.

Taking the cassette he had just purchased out of the other plastic bag, he tossed the books onto the bed and slid the videocassette from its black plastic sleeve. He stuffed the tape into the VCR and sat back on the bed with the remotes to both the VCR and the TV.

Once the TV came to life, static filled the screen. He pushed the PLAY button on the VCR remote.

Static was replaced by pure blackness. Ryan worked the fast-forward until the screen gave way to rolling hills, a forest and a car speeding along a narrow roadway.

He was surprised and relieved. The picture quality was no worse than a movie taped from TV. The time code bar clicked away in the bottom corner of the screen.

The car continued its ascent up the winding pathway until the camera revealed a sinister looking manse sitting atop the hill's crest. A bolt of lightning cracked the night sky but no sound effect gave it audible life.

When the car stopped a man and a woman got out and approached the house. The man looked familiar. Ryan had seen him before but could not place him. Maybe he had been in one of Lamberto Bava's pictures, or maybe in Michele Soavi's *Dellamorte Dellamore.*

The woman was an attractive blonde actress with long legs and high cheekbones. She was interchangeable with most European actresses.

When they spoke Ryan had no idea what they were saying. But, having spent half his life watching horror films, he knew they no doubt were discussing the ugly house, which was more than likely an inheritance of some sort.

A butler with a withered hand sheathed in a black glove greeted them at the front entrance and quickly ushered them into the house. The butler too looked familiar to Ryan, but he couldn't place the actor.

The couple took in the grand spectacle of the giant front room while Ryan again leaned on the fast forward button, searching out a little of the red sauce for which Sacchetti was famous.

He stopped fast-forwarding as the camera lingered on the blonde woman's naked body while she showered.

Ryan smiled. Sacchetti never passed on an opportunity to linger on a little bare skin.

Suddenly, a hand grabbed the woman and she screamed. He winced at the horrid sound that came out of her mouth. The woman's scream was croaky, without substance and obviously not filled with terror. Then he realized the scream had yet to be properly dubbed.

The woman turned. It was only the main actor, the one Ryan couldn't place. They kissed, then made love under the shower.

Fast-forwarding further, he stopped on a scene of the man roaming in the dark of what looked like a family crypt. He showed his flashlight beam all around, reacting to non-existent sound effects.

Stumbling through the darkness, the man found a sarcophagus. Its lid was cracked. There was writing on its stone surface. The writing was in English, no doubt filmed with the American film market in mind, but the man read the words in Italian.

Ryan read the words aloud.

"The time of the demon lord is here. The time to free the demons from hell is now. There is no more room in hell. It is time for the demons to rise and walk the Earth."

The whole scene was surreal. Smoke billowed in the air around the man and Ryan thought the air in the room was becoming smoky too. It was no longer cold, but warm. Like a closed off crypt. The air in the hotel room was musty and stained with the stench of death and decay.

On the screen the man reacted to a noise, only Ryan heard the sound this time. It had come from the closet near the room's bathroom. The man on the TV seemed to be staring in the direction of the closet.

A steady thump of pain was filling Ryan's head, building in its intensity as the time code in the corner of the screen sped up. As the numbers clicked by faster, the pain grew more excruciating. He felt lightheaded and nauseated, like the world around him was going soft around the edges and falling just out of reach.

Investigating the noise, the man on the screen crept into the darkness, only now the room in which Ryan sat was dark too, dark like the crypt. No light came through the windows, just more darkness.

Ryan was lost in the film. He heard the man's footfalls and they sounded nearby.

The thumping pain was pounding directly behind his eyes. It was growing, spreading. It felt as if his brain was on fire.

Moving slowly toward the source of the sound, the man flashed his light onto the lid of another stone coffin. Again the written words and again Ryan read them aloud.

"The time of the demon lord is here. The time to free the demons from hell is now. There is no more room in hell. It is time for the demons to rise and walk the Earth."

The sarcophagus lid slowly slid open. The sound effect boomed in the room and intensified the pain in Ryan's head.

The sarcophagus was empty.

Without warning, the stone lid of a sarcophagus behind the man burst open. A demon, the butler with the withered hand, but now disfigured with scabby brown skin and fangs, leapt forward and jumped on the man's back. The demon butler sank his teeth deep into the man's neck.

At the same moment as the attack on screen, the closet door next to the bathroom in the room burst open and the same kind of disfigured demon from the movie was on Ryan, biting deeply into his neck.

In his final moments, before the world went black, Ryan finally placed the two actors in the movie.

Looking a bit older and grayer around the temples than the last time he had seen him in a picture accompanying an interview in Blood Scream Magazine, the man who had arrived at the manse with the attractive blonde woman was Paolo Sacchetti.

With hair neatly trimmed and face cleanly shaven; the butler with the withered hand in the black glove was the dealer who just sold Ryan the tape.

* * *

"Yo, Ryan. You in here, buddy?" Eddie flipped on the lights. The room was empty.

"Damn."

"You think he's all right?" Kristi was holding Eddie's hand.

"Something must be wrong for him to miss meeting Jack Dubose. His stuff's still here." Eddie nodded at Ryan's bed.

"Maybe he got sick," Kristi suggested.

"Hey, buddy, are you in there?" Eddie rapped gently on the bathroom door. "Are you sick?" When he got no response he opened the door. The bathroom was empty.

"You sure you never saw him in the dealer's room?"

"Never saw him," she assured.

"I kept watching for him over at the Screamies table to get his poster signed, but he never showed up."

"He wasn't there."

"This ain't like Ryan." The concern in Eddie's face and in his voice was sincere.

"Should we worry?"

"I don't know." Eddie dropped his new purchases on his bed next to the model kits.

"Maybe he just went to get something to eat."

"No, he would have waited for me."

"What, are you guys joined at the hip? Share the same brain?"

"No."

"Then it is possible that he just went out to grab something to eat? Or maybe he met someone too, and he's up in her room, right?"

Neither suggestion was entirely out of the question, Eddie admitted to himself. It just wasn't like Ryan to go off without a word.

"Maybe we should just stay up here and wait for him." Kristi slid the strap of her art tube over her head and set the plastic tube on the floor.

"Whatever will we do?" Eddie asked coyly.

"I think we can find some way to entertain ourselves." Kristi smiled and pulled the zombie tee-shirt over her head.

* * *

Ryan watched silently, saw everything from the crack of the closet door.

His body had changed, transformed. For the first time in his life he felt powerful, strong. There was an insatiable hunger burning deep inside him.

He watched the two bodies roll about on the bed. The raven-haired girl had milky white skin. Ryan could smell the blood coursing through her body beneath the flawless flesh. Could practically see it flowing through the blue veins under her soft flesh.

Ryan imagined biting into the velvety soft flesh, of devouring it and gorging on the crimson flow that would spray from beneath. He could almost taste the hot coppery wash as it would fill his mouth.

When he could stand it no longer, Ryan sprang from his hiding place.

* * *

"Stop it!" the girl snapped, pushing him away. "I'm not that type of girl."

"Sure you are, kitten, or you never would have agreed to come up to my room."

Michael Overton was feeling good. The cocktails in the hotel bar had helped to take the edge off of having been stuck signing autographs for six hours straight. He signed so many headshots and stills and posters from the *Dead Things* series he wanted to puke.

"Maybe you should just let me off on the next floor."

He looked at the girl. She was another groupie who had just been a little kid when the original *Dead Things* flick was released. What's it been, over twenty years ago already? It depressed him to think he had a daughter at home older than her.

"Gimmie some smooches, sweetness."

"Cut it out!" She pushed him away. "I thought you wanted to run lines with me and see if there's a part for me in your next movie."

He smiled. They always fell for the old "part in the next movie" ploy. He wished there was a "next movie." If there was, he sure as hell wouldn't be attending this miserable convention. "What I think, kitten, is that when we get to my room, we're gonna get real close and chummy."

Tears welled in the corners of her eyes.

The actor put a finger on her chin and said, "What I think is that I'm gonna give you a good test-drive around the block, then drop you off in front of somebody else's house. Get me?"

The girl looked humiliated and furious.

"You go to hell."

"Come on, now you're sounding like my wife, kissy-face." He made a grab for her.

"I said stop it!" She jerked away from him and stopped the elevator car. Her hand hovered dangerously close to the big red Emergency button.

"Touch me again and I'll have you arrested."

"Take it easy, kitten. I was only fooling."

"Yeah, fooling. I'm getting off on the next floor." She pressed the button for the fifteenth floor and engaged the car into motion.

* * *

When the elevator doors opened, Michael Overton sighed disgustedly.

"The costume contest's tomorrow, freaks. That's when I'm judging, not tonight." The trio of fans was made up like demons. Their skin was discolored, brownish and covered in sores and scabs and their mouths were full of razor sharp teeth. They smelled horrible too. "You guys do know all that goop on your faces will eventually cause bad skin irritations, right?"

He noticed that two of the trio were naked, and one of them was female.

"I might be coerced into awarding you a first place prize trophy if you want to escort me up to my room, little sweet-something." He put his arm around the demon girl.

"You're disgusting." When the girl tried to push past the two male demons they grabbed her. Their teeth sank into her flesh. They fell on top of her into the elevator car, gorging on the red spray from the gaping hole in her neck.

"Hey, freaks!"

The female demon bared her teeth and attacked the actor.

Slowly, the elevator doors shut behind the desperate cries of the actor and the girl.

* * *

The hunger drove them. When the elevator doors opened on another floor, they found a waiter delivering room service.

Further down the hallway they found party-goers staggering back to their rooms, intoxicated and easily overcome.

When a room door opened to the commotion in the hallway, the demons fed again.

Their numbers grew rapidly.

They moved through the stairwells and service hallways. A maintenance man, a cleaning lady preparing for the morning shift, another waiter and a security man joined their demonic ranks.

They continued to feed. Their contamination continued to spread, continued to awaken the dead. With each feast, their numbers continued to multiply.

Finally they found the night, found the solace and cover of the darkness.

Into the city they fled, scurrying, hiding. They sought cover before dawn.

* * *

Marc roamed the dealer's room but nothing caught his eye.

The Frightmare Horror Convention was turning out to be a major non-event. Nothing was happening. He figured it was because of the Demon Con down in San Diego the month before.

Twenty-seven people were still missing; hotel guests, employees, many of the regular convention dealers and even the guy who starred in all those old, cheesy *Dead Things* movies.

He had heard from a friend who had attended Demon Con that a number of the rooms looked like slaughterhouses. Blood on the walls, on the ceilings, guts strewn all about but no bodies. It was like all those people had been butchered to pieces and then carried off.

Or maybe they turned into zombies and walked away. Marc just shook his head.

The Internet buzz was saying the Demon Con fiasco was putting the entire convention scene out of business. Many cons were canceling and the ones that were still running were having a decrease in attendance, as well as an increase in dealer and guest no-shows.

Marc had hoped to meet Jack Dubose, as well as legends like Herschell Gordon Lewis and Ted V. Mikels, but all canceled the Frightmare Horror Con at the last minute.

Did that result in Marc getting a break on his ticket to get in? Hell no, he thought angrily. He still had to pay full price for what amounted to a half-assed convention full of no-shows. There were hardly any dealers around for him to spend his money on.

He came upon a table full of bootleg videos. Marc smirked. Of course the video bootleggers would still show. They couldn't afford to miss a show.

Marc began perusing the handwritten titles on the video spines when the dealer behind the table spoke to him.

"Hey, man," the dealer said getting up from a metal folding chair. "You dig on Italian cannibal flicks?"

The Room

When he awoke, a sharp pain pounded within Quentin Lansing's skull. He felt dizzy when he sat upright. He rubbed his temples and fought the wave of nausea that tried to overtake him.

"We thought you were never going to wake up."

The voice sounded tired, but familiar. It was a voice Quentin had not heard in a long time.

"Cyndi? Cyndi Watson?"

"Prescott now," the blonde woman said from the wicker chair. She picked at her wedding band with a long red fingernail.

"How's it hanging, boss?"

"Bert?"

"It's me." The big man in the rocking chair offered a lopsided smile.

"It's just like old times, huh, Quint?" Cyndi asked quietly.

It was like a dream, or some bizarre hallucination. Quentin rubbed his eyes, then his temples again.

He had not seen Cyndi Watson, now Prescott, or Bert Simmons since they parted ways after graduating high school.

Cyndi was still attractive, Quentin observed. She still had a nice body. She would always be the peppy cheerleader. But the creases at the corners of her eyes made her look tired and old.

"What the hell is going on here?" he croaked. His throat was sore and his mouth dry.

"Beats us, boss," Bert said from the rocking chair. "It's no place either of us ever seen before. How about you?"

Nineteen years had never been crueler to a man than in the case of Big Bert Simmons, the high school football star. The hair on his head was all but a memory and his body was mostly stomach. He still looked as stupid as Quentin remembered him looking in high school.

Quentin looked away from Bert to take in his surroundings.

It was a simple room, roughly ten feet by twelve feet in size. It was just big enough to accommodate the chairs Cyndi and Bert sat on and the long coffee table in the room's center. The top of the coffee table was bare. It had cabinet doors on either end.

Landscapes in simple wood frames adorned the plain white walls.

There were no windows, but there was a door. Beige shag carpet covered the floor.

The ceiling was maybe ten feet high. Higher than most, Quentin thought. The fluorescent light fixture above provided the only light in the room. It was impossible to tell if it were day or night.

"I've never seen it before in my life," Quentin finally said.

He steadied himself against the wall and stood. He made his way to the door. Reaching for the knob he gave it a hard twist.

"We already tried that, boss," Bert offered.

Quentin tugged on the door handle fiercely then pounded on its surface.

"This is ridiculous," he said between clenched teeth. "Hey!" he shouted to whoever might hear on the other side. "The joke's over. Open the door!" He beat upon the door until his knuckles were red and aching. He continued beating until finally he grew tired and abandoned the effort. Turning,

Quentin slid down the face of the door to the carpeted floor, cradling his painful hands.

* * *

"All I remember," Cyndi started quietly, "was driving home and thinking about what I was going to make for dinner, chicken or pork chops."

Bert made a snorting noise, like a laugh swallowed up in a sigh.

"I was at a stop light when a car pulled up next to me. I didn't notice it at first, but then I had the weird feeling I was being watched. I looked over but I couldn't see the driver. His windows were tinted black." She fell silent a moment and hit the arm of the wicker chair with the open palm of one hand before continuing.

"When the light turned green I don't remember going anywhere. I remember the light changing, but nothing after. It's all just a blank until I woke up here, in this chair. You were both here, still asleep, when I woke up."

Looking around, Cyndi shuddered. A phantom creep had suddenly slid down her spine and made the hairs on her neck stand at attention.

The scenario of her abduction haunted Quentin in that he too was unable to recall his own. There was a whole slice of time, a part of his life, which was nothing more than a blank, a dead zone where he seemed to have ceased existing.

He remembered taking Ted Danning out for drinks in hopes of sealing their deal, then excusing himself to the restroom. After going to the bathroom he recalled nothing else. It was all a big black void, until waking up a short while ago.

Surely to God Ted Danning wondered where he was after a time and came looking for him. He would have had to see Quentin being carried out of the bar. Somebody would have seen something.

He looked at his wrist but his watch was gone. He turned to face Bert.

"What about you? Do you remember anything?"

"Pretty much the same deal as you guys, boss. Don't know who snatched me or how or when or why. I was working late at the lot, catching up on some paperwork. I run the Ford Dealership in Clarkston for my father-in-law who…"

"Clarkston," Quentin interrupted, cutting Bert off in mid-sentence.

"Yeah," Bert said slowly. "It's the one right off the high-way."

"But Clarkston is two hundred miles away."

"Away from where?" Bert asked irritably.

None of this was making any sense. The more Quentin thought about it, the more his already aching head pounded harder.

"Two hundred miles from Millwood," he responded in a small voice.

A quiet fell over the room.

"For all we know," Cyndi began. "We're being held in Clarkston and Millwood is two hundred miles away."

"This is insane," Quentin yelled, unable to accept his current circumstances. Getting to his feet he began feeling around the wall with open palms, looking for a secret switch that would open a secret door in their prison.

"Look, we need to try and keep our cool, boss." Bert was trying to sound reasonable. "This is crazy, and we don't really know how long we've been here, but if we've really been gone any substantial amount of time, that means people are looking for us at this very minute, right?"

It sounded reasonable. Yes, Cyndi's husband no doubt had the authorities already searching for his missing wife. Although Quentin had been alone since things didn't work out with Diane two years ago, Mr. Dugan, his boss at the firm, would have people looking for him. Hell, if word got back that he blew the Danning deal, Dugan would have hit men out looking for him. Yes, people would be looking for them.

But where would they be looking? What if they were hundreds of miles away from where they had each been abducted? What if there were no clues? Whoever snatched each of them obviously knew what they were doing.

Bert Simmons' words did sound very reasonable. At this moment, people would be searching for them. But the idea did little to instill any kind of hope in the people held captive in the room.

"Christ," Quentin mumbled to no one in particular.

* * *

"What's a room?" Quentin asked.

"What's a what," Bert mumbled.

"What's a room? What's it made of? A room is constructed of two-by-fours and drywall, right?"

"I guess," Bert answered, sitting up and leaning toward Quentin.

"Of course it is. And between the walls would be insulation and wiring. It will either lead to another room or to an outside wall, which could be made of brick and mortar, or plywood and siding, right?" Quentin stood.

"We could break out of here. Just go right through the wall. We could use the legs of the coffee table like picks if we had to and dig a hole out."

Bert and Cyndi didn't look convinced.

"It's a chance," Quentin said loudly.

"A fat chance," Bert said tiredly. "Whatever's behind the drywall is solid, boss. It's not two-by-four studs."

"It's just studs and drywall," Quentin retorted fiercely. He refused to let the big man's pessimism and negativity take away his tiny sparkle of hope.

"Watch this." To prove his theory Quentin reared back and kicked the wall with all his might.

A white-hot pain exploded throughout his foot and thundered up his leg. The wall was solid as steel behind the drywall.

* * *

From where he sat on the floor, Quentin had been able to pick a hole big enough in the drywall to reveal a solid metal backing. Quietly he sat and picked chunks of the sheet rock from where it had been glued to the steel.

Frustrated, he tugged the carpet until it gave and pulled free. Popping free from where it had been glued down, a large corner of carpeting tore away from the floor.

There was no padding beneath the carpet. Like behind the drywall facade, solid metal stared back at him.

* * *

"I think," Cyndi began speaking barely above a whisper. "That we're all dead."

Quentin watched as she began to sob. Cyndi looked haggard and ugly when she cried. The tears mixing with make-up gave her the appearance of a clown whose face was melting off his skull.

"For Christ's sake, shut up!" Bert barked. Eyes bulging, filling with anger immediately, the big man looked like a crazed, caged animal.

"I'm never going to see my babies again," she said between choking sobs.

"We ain't dead," Bert shouted fiercely. Springing up from the rocking chair he reached toward Cyndi and grabbed her arm and shook her violently. The frail woman looked like she would break to pieces if he continued shaking her.

"If we're dead," Bert screamed down at the sobbing woman. "Then why am I so damn hungry? You think we'd be starving if we were dead?" He pushed her away and let her sob into her hands by herself.

* * *

"Oh my, God," Cyndi whispered.

Quentin, still picking away at the drywall to reveal more of the metal wall underneath, looked up to see if Cyndi and Bert's search for nourishment in the room's four corners had produced a crumb or morsel of some long discarded, stale food.

"Now this is damn weird," Bert offered, momentarily forgetting the painful grumbling in his stomach. Scratching his head he looked over at the former football captain for guidance.

Quentin's heart began beating faster when he saw what Cyndi laid on the top of the coffee table.

"It was in the back of one of the cabinets of the coffee table," she said.

Untouched and unopened, the leather bound Dalton High School yearbook stared back at them from the surface of the coffee table.

"He did it," Cyndi said and began laughing. The laughter was devoid of humor or mirth. It was the laughter of someone who was dangerously close to losing her mind.

"What the hell are you talking about?" Bert growled. He looked as if he wanted to punch the woman to make her stop laughing.

"He said he'd get us. You remember, don't you? He swore he would get us back." The hideous laughter came again, between chocking sobs, sounding like fingernails scrapping down a chalkboard. "He got us real good." Tears were running down Cyndi's cheeks.

Robert Freese

"Who?" Bert demanded, again grabbing Cyndi's arm and shaking her.

"You know damn well who!" Cyndi spat. Her lips formed a wide, grotesque smile.

Bert slapped her across the face with an open palm.

"Kenny Michaels!" Cyndi screamed at him. She repeated the name over and over until Bert raised his hand to slap her again and she quieted down, drawing into herself on the wicker chair.

Quentin felt his stomach flop.

For a long moment the name remained lost to Bert. When it finally came to him, Bert's face went ashen, draining of all expression.

"The junk-man did this," Bert asked in a monotone whisper. He began to move about the room in frantic circles.

"I mean," he said in a louder voice, running his fingers over the top of his sweaty head. "There's no way the junk-man could have done this. There ain't no way in hell."

"It's him, Bert!" Cyndi hollered.

"It can't be him because the junk-man's dead!" Bert Simmons roared.

* * *

"The junk-man likes you," Quentin teased.

"Shut up," Cyndi said, blushing. She was shoving books into her locker.

"What's up," Big Bert asked, sidling up to the row of lockers next to his friends.

"The junk-man has the hots for Cyndi," Quentin said mockingly. "He sent her a love letter. He wants to take her out on a date."

"Yeah, and Quint's jealous so he's being a jerk," Cyndi replied with a wicked smile.

"You better watch it, boss. The junk-man's liable to sweep her off her feet and move her up to his daddy's salvage yard." Bert wore a big horse grin across his face.

"They'll be crowned king and queen of the trash heap."

"You guys are real funny," Cyndi said irritably, slamming her locker shut. "Hysterical in fact." She turned away from the boys.

"Hey wait a minute," Quentin said. He caught Cyndi by the sleeve of her blouse before she got away. "I got a great idea."

* * *

"He's not dead." Quentin tasted bile in the back of his throat when he spoke.

"He died up at that Saint-whatever hospital. He hung himself is what I heard," Bert retorted, still pacing.

"He didn't die," Quentin insisted.

"We did that to him," Cyndi said. She pulled her knees to her chest and suddenly felt very cold.

"We didn't do anything!" Bert bellowed.

* * *

The plan was simple. Cyndi agreed to go out with Kenny, as much as she detested the idea. It was difficult for her to remember to call him by his real name. Kenny Michaels had been christened "the junk-man" in grade school after the kids found out how his father made his living.

The night was awkward and uncomfortable, but Cyndi finally got Kenny to take her up to Sutter's Point, a secluded make-out haven.

Once there, Quentin and Bert sprang from hiding spots and before Kenny Michaels knew what happened, they had him locked in the trunk of his own car.

Kenny kicked and screamed and cursed, beat on the lid of the trunk from within. He sounded like a hysterical child desperately trying to escape from the dark.

Laughing and piling into Quentin's car, they left him.

* * *

Quentin felt nauseated again.

"We left him up there for three days," Cyndi whispered. Fat tears still streamed down her cheeks. "They said he was in complete shock when that state trooper finally found him. His hands were bloody shreds from beating on the inside of the trunk."

"This is a load of crap," Bert said, cursing under his breath.

"He's up there," Cyndi whispered, peering up at the high ceiling. "He's watching us. He's waited all this time and now Kenny is going to set the record straight."

Quentin and Bert looked up at the ceiling. Neither said a word, each feeling the peering eyes upon them from beyond the room's six sides.

"I can feel him watching us."

* * *

Quentin had no way of knowing how much time had passed since he first woke up, but it felt like days. Time ceased to exist in the room. The only thing that existed with any real substance was the past, which hung in the air like a thick, noxious cloud.

At different times, each nodded off to sleep, only to awake and find they were still captives in the room.

Nothing changed; time stayed frozen in the room.

There were no outside noises, no voices or honking horns or squealing tires or barking dogs.

Stillness permeated the sour, dead air.

Then, quite suddenly, an alien sound broke the omnipresent silence. A loud pneumatic hissing thundered within the room, like the world was suddenly moving, possibly breaking apart and crumbling around them.

"What the hell?" Bert cried, jumping out of the rocking chair.

The wall Quentin was leaning against began moving forward. The room suddenly seemed to be shrinking as it pushed him along the floor. He tried to brace his legs but there was nothing to brace them against.

"I just want to see my babies again!" Cyndi screamed hysterically at the ceiling. "Please stop it. I'm sorry, Kenny. I'm so sorry." Her sobbing pleas were drowned out under the churning sounds of a grinding engine.

Continuing to shrink, the ceiling finally buckled and shattered. When the light fixture exploded, it rained down electrical sparks and broken glass. Soon the ceiling planking and two-by-fours came crashing down upon them.

Beyond the false ceiling was the night, dark and clear and full of stars. A rush of cool air blew in on them and was then sucked out in all the dust and falling debris.

The world seemed empty, as if no one existed beyond the slowly dwindling confines of the room. The entire quiet world was made up three desperately shrieking individuals who shared a dark moment in the past.

* * *

Even after their screams died away, the jaws of the giant salvage crusher refused to stop moving until the opposite walls almost met, and the contents of the room and its occupants were nearly crushed flat.

Scream Queen

Graham Talby worked steadily, his fingers gliding over the keyboard without pause, using words and sentences to create scenes. He worked as if his efforts meant something.

INTERIOR, Sorority House bathroom

The bathroom is steamy. The blast of the shower fills the room. The camera takes on the Point Of View of THE SLAYER, as he enters the bathroom. The mirror is too steamed over to reveal much of THE SLAYER'S features as he walks past, but it is obvious THE SLAYER wears a mask to conceal his face. The closer he gets to the shower, the more defined the figure behind the shower curtain becomes.

Inside the shower stall, MELANIE is standing under the hot water. Her head is tilted back slightly as she softly caresses her body with a soapy washrag under the hot streams.

* * *

Sure, Talby thought, *just like all women do when they take a shower.* His fingers continued to play over the keys, the pace never slackening.

* * *

The lights in the bathroom suddenly go out, leaving MELANIE and THE SLAYER in the dark. MELANIE panics. She has soap stinging her eyes. Blindly she reaches for the faucet handles and turns the shower off.

MELANIE
"Hello? Who's there?"

There is no response. MELANIE reaches out for a towel and wraps it around her body.

From the POV of THE SLAYER, the camera is only a couple feet away from the shower stall. THE SLAYER is close enough to reach out and touch MELANIE'S hand when she reaches for the towel.

MELANIE
"This is not funny. You guys need to cut it out. I have an important date with Chet Parks tonight and I have to get ready."

MELANIE gets no response. Hurriedly, she takes another towel and begins drying her hair.

From the POV of THE SLAYER, a hunting knife is raised into the camera frame and THE SLAYER begins to

* * *

Wait a minute. Talby re-read the last couple lines. Something in the direction didn't make sense.

"She has soap stinging her eyes," he mumbled when he found the inconsistency in his script. "When the lights go out, she turns the water off but she has soap in her eyes, so she grabs for her towel and doesn't wipe the soap from her eyes first." He stared at the computer screen for several long moments contemplating the actions of his character and chewing the bottom of his lip.

"Screw it," he finally decided. No one watching a movie called *Sorority Death House* was going to care about a little flub like that. Not as long as the girl stays naked. The director could fix it, if he even noticed the flub. Besides, he reasoned, fans of these kinds of flicks expected stuff like that; it was part of the fun in watching them. It gave the fans something to gripe about and pick apart in movie chat rooms and on-line blogs. Everyone loves to be a critic.

Finding the place in the script where he'd stopped; Talby resumed the action as his fingers began tapping the keys.

* * *

From the POV of THE SLAYER, a hunting knife is raised into the camera frame and THE SLAYER begins moving toward the shower stall.

MELANIE continues to dry herself until she hears the creak of a floorboard and knows somebody is in the dark bathroom with her.

MELANIE
"Quit it, right now! You're not being funny!"

MELANIE grabs the shower curtain and swishes it to one side.

From the POV of Melanie, the bathroom is empty. It appears that no one else is in the bathroom.

MELANIE
"I guess it's just my imagination."

MELANIE shuts the shower curtain to finish drying her body. As soon as she does, the hunting knife is plunged through the curtain into her back.

MELANIE struggles and tries to scream but she is in shock. The hunting knife goes into her again and again. Spinning around in the stall, MELANIE becomes entangled in the shower curtain. THE SLAYER continues to stab MELANIE as her body becomes wrapped up in the shower curtain.

Blood splashes across the tiles and floor and all over the steamed-up bathroom mirror.

Losing her balance, MELANIE falls forward onto the bathroom floor. Her body is still.

The screen goes to black. The camera begins to track backward, slowly revealing the iris of MELANIE'S eye. Then her blood-splattered face is revealed. The camera continues to track back until the entire bathroom is revealed, with MELA-NIE dead on the floor.

THE SLAYER comes into frame; his masked face is shown. He kneels at MELANIE'S body and wipes the blood off the hunting knife using the shower curtain. When the knife is clean THE SLAYER gets up and leaves the bathroom.

* * *

"Thank you, Mr. Hitchcock," Talby mumbled, finishing the scene. Sitting back in his chair he cracked his knuckles. It was already noon. Danny would be expecting Talby to join him for lunch in his cramped little office.

He sighed. Everything about New Hollywood Pictures was cramped.

Danny would want to know about the script. The big producer would have a million questions about how far Talby had gotten and if he was including all the specific scenes Danny wanted.

To be honest, Talby thought, it wasn't much of a script. It was derivative of dozens of other babes-and-blades slasher flicks made over the past twenty years. But that wasn't the point. For what it was, the script for *Sorority Death House* served its purpose. It delivered the gore and the scares and the boobs just as Danny demanded when he gave Talby the assignment a week ago. Like everything else at New Hollywood Pictures, the script didn't have to be good or original, it just had to be finished on time.

Tiredly, Talby got up from his desk and stretched until his back popped. Then he left his little office to meet Danny Owens for lunch.

* * *

Although the larger of the two offices, Danny's office seemed to be the smaller as it was crammed corner to corner with boxes full of promotional materials and overflowing file cabinets. Sometimes, when he was in Danny's office, Talby got the feeling that the four walls were closing in on him.

Danny was already biting into his meatball sub when he entered. Talby had gotten tired of sub sandwiches long ago but as long as Danny kept picking up the lunch tab, he would keep eating them. He sat opposite Danny and tore into the white takeout bag containing his hero sub.

"How's the script looking?" Danny asked after swallowing a giant glob of half-chewed meat and bread. He chased it with a long swig of diet soda. There was a smear of red sauce on his chin.

"It's looking like a script," answered Talby noncommittally. *It looks exactly like the last six scripts I wrote*, he thought. It seemed New Hollywood Pictures was content to keep cranking out the same movie over and over again, as if no one ever noticed.

"Cut the smart-ass bit. I need it done by the end of the week to give it to Lou Michaels. He's coming up Friday to take a look at it. He thinks that based on the title alone we can get some up-front money from his Japanese investors." Danny punctuated his words by tearing free another chunk of sandwich.

Irritably, Talby said, "It will be done. Have I ever let you down before and not delivered?"

Danny Owens just looked at him. Danny's maw was full and his jaws were working mechanically to grind up the food inside to make room for more.

When they were done eating, Talby crumbled up the wax paper his sub sandwich had come wrapped in and pitched it toward an overflowing wastebasket. It hit the wall, bounced away and never even touched the rim of the basket.

"That's why you're a writer," Danny said, snorting a laugh. He took a couple folders and placed them in the center of his cluttered desk.

"We need to find some girls for this picture so Lou will have some faces to pitch to his investors along with the title and script." He flipped the top folder open and took half the stack of 8X10 headshots, passing the rest of the stack to Talby.

All the girls looked the same to him. They were young and pretty, but they had a generic, fresh off the assembly line look to them. Some he recognized from past films. Some had appeared in movies he had written, his words having contorted their beauty into horribly wounded victims or wildly mutated monsters.

No one photo stood out more than the others, but every third or fourth one he put in a separate stack because that was what Danny expected of him. Truth be told, he would rather be back in his office pounding out the clichés for his script than sitting with Danny, poring over headshots.

"What about Jodi?" Danny asked. He held a black and white glamour photo of Jodi Craven between two greasy fingers.

187

"Not a chance," Talby answered. He didn't look up, just talked as he kept flipping through his stack of photos. "I heard she signed the cable deal, hosting that Saturday night horror show. She's got twenty-two shows guaranteed with a percentage of the tie-in merchandise, the posters and tee-shirts and calendars and whatever. I hear she got the whole deal. At this point, she probably wouldn't do it for scale let alone as a favor. Forget it." He reached for his soda and drank.

"I'll be damned." Danny wasn't talking to him in particular. He was just talking. He put the photo back with the others while his fat fingers continued to search the pile.

"Tina Langdon?" he asked.

"I think she's still pissed off at you."

"Oh, yeah."

During the production of *Catholic School Girl Massacre*, Ms. Langdon had a problem performing her contractual nude scene. She wanted a closed set and the show's director declined her request. Danny had been called down to the set to settle the dispute. The matter was resolved when Danny agreed to clear away the crew and shoot the scene himself. After four grueling hours, Danny informed the actress and her scene-mate that none of the footage he had gotten was usable and that they would have to shoot the same scene the following day. Tina Langdon had been enraged and walked off the set. Danny had to hire her back for more money and no nude scenes.

Talby shook his head. If only the girl knew that Danny had every frame of footage from that shooting day on tape and that he ran it for friends for laughs, she would probably come hunting his big grizzly bear hide for her trophy wall.

"How about Traci Dutch," Talby offered half-heartedly.

"Not right for the part. Traci's too funny for a piece like this. I like to use her as bimbo comedy relief and a little," Danny wiggled his body like a hippo trying to hula dance to finish his thought. "This new picture is serious and doesn't have room for any funny stuff."

Serious? Talby was suddenly afraid he was going to burst out laughing and squirt soda out his nose. *Serious?* Did he hear that correctly? *I must be working on the wrong script,* he thought. *The script I'm working on has a group of sorority pledges and their boyfriends staying the night in a haunted sorority house with a killer on the loose. Serious?*

"Robyn Monroe?" Danny's eyes moved over the color glossy of the blonde actress like a hawk sizing up its prey before swooping down for the kill.

"A husband and two kids. She's been out of the game for a while. It must be something, to have a real life so you don't have to do this crap for a living anymore." Talby finished his soda.

"What a shame," Danny said. Finishing his stack he put the photos to one side and picked up another stack.

"What about some of the new girls?" Talby suggested. He took the photos of the new girls the talent agents sent regularly in hopes of drumming up jobs for their new clients.

Wendy McClain, Suzy Downs, Allison Haven, Jenny Stryker, Kathy Deeds, all of them were the same; pretty, wholesome faces and a desire to attain fame and fortune in a town that ate little girls for breakfast.

But that was not the point, he thought quietly, flipping through the glossies. The point was, they needed talent for their movie, and the girls were whom they had to choose. They served their purpose.

Most would get a chance to make pictures at New Hollywood, especially if they could remember their lines, show up on time and not come to work hung over or strung out. It was much like the jobs they had waiting tables until they were given their big break.

Big break. Talby thought those were two of the most misrepresented words in the English language when they were stuck together.

When he was a little kid, he spent his summers sequestered away from the world, tucked safely away inside the air-conditioned bellies of the old palace theatres, watching movie after movie, until the school bell rang again in the fall.

He would sit and watch, eyes big as pie plates, and dream that one day he would move to Hollywood and make pictures that people would want to see, pictures they would be willing to stand in line in the rain to see.

Dropping out of USC after a spec script he wrote was optioned, Graham Talby was invited to take up residency with New Hollywood Pictures. He got along well enough with Danny Owens and the merry-go-round of people who came and went. Most were just glitter and flash with a smile and an unfulfilled promise. He got his cramped little office and out of date computer and figured that one day he would look back at his time with New Hollywood Pictures with fondness. He thought he'd arrived, that he was on his way and that he had finally gotten his own big break. Fame and fortune were surely to follow.

Nine years and a dozen scripts later, Talby was no further along than when he was a kid, dreaming giant dreams and watching the big screen.

Big breaks were a load of crap. So was fame and fortune. A dozen produced scripts and he still scrambled to pay the rent on his crummy apartment every month.

It was enough to make him stop on occasion and curse himself for ever dreaming. Instead of writing scripts for movies people stood in line in the rain to see, he wrote scripts for movies that were the last thing most people saw before they fell asleep in front of the television at night.

But in the big picture, Talby knew the score. He knew his place. New Hollywood Pictures needed scripts to make movies and he provided the scripts. In that regard, he served his purpose.

"Stop the presses," Danny said, snapping Talby out of his reverie. He flipped the headshot around like a flashcard.

She was a petite blonde with a nice figure and breasts that could stop an oncoming tractor trailer. Like the others, she had a fresh, wholesome look and she wore a nice smile.

The name on the back of the photo was Annette Cage. One Mr. Herbert Slayton, who served also as her personal make-up consultant and agent, represented her. Underneath their names there was a contact number and a line that read, "Now that you've seen two of my big talents, call and ask about my third."

"Third?" Talby asked. A crooked grin stretched across Danny's double chin. The look on his face said Ms. Cage already had the job. Talby didn't try to convince Danny otherwise.

Interviews were set up at various times for Annette and six other aspiring actresses to come in and read for parts. Betty Coogan, New Hollywood's receptionist, made calls to each of the girls' agents and arranged readings. Ms. Cage was scheduled to arrive for her reading Thursday morning.

* * *

EXTERIOR- Backyard of the Sorority House

LISA is running across the backyard, which is little more than an unkempt, weed filled lot. She trips over some rusted yard furniture and screams. THE SLAYER seems to be catching up with her, even though she is running and he is walking.

Robert Freese

Picking herself up, LISA runs up onto the back porch and beats furiously on the back door.

LISA
"Open the door! Melanie, Tina...Oh, God, Christopher, open the door!"

There is a creaking sound. LISA screams and turns around but THE SLAYER is gone.

Tears stream down LISA'S face. She moves off the back porch to see where THE SLAYER has gone. She hears another creaking sound.

When LISA turns around to return to the back porch, the bodies of TINA and GARY fall from above. TINA and GARY are both dead. Their bodies are tied up in bloody bed sheets and they swing over the edge of the back porch, blocking LISA'S way into the house.

Nearby, THE SLAYER appears. LISA screams and runs around to the front of the house.

Rather than run immediately to the front door, LISA runs to the car they all arrived in. The door is locked, but she struggles with the handle to try and open it. Her struggling causes the dead body of CHRISTOPHER, her boyfriend, to hit the car window from inside. His throat has been slit from ear to ear.

LISA
"God, no! Christopher!"

LISA screams and runs toward the front of the sorority house.

* * *

"And of course, nobody hears her scream," Talby muttered sarcastically as his fingers punched the words that put his heroine back into the charnel house of terror.

* * *

The front door of the sorority house is jammed. THE SLAYER appears from around the corner of the house. Although still just walking, THE SLAYER seems to be approaching quickly. Screaming, struggling, LISA finally pushes the door open and enters the house. She slams the door shut just in time for THE SLAYER'S hunting knife to miss her and bury itself into the door.

INTERIOR- Sorority House

LISA is leaning on the front door. She screams frantically as THE SLAYER beats on the door from outside. Straining to keep the door shut, LISA finally runs to the stairwell when she can no longer hold the door closed.

The door crashes inward. THE SLAYER fills the doorway, his outline silhouetted with the glowing moon behind him.

LISA bolts upstairs.

From the POV of THE SLAYER, he moves quickly, stalking her up the stairs.

At the top of the stairs LISA trips and falls. The floor in front of the bathroom is wet. Desperately, she scrambles to get into the bathroom and throws the door shut behind her.

INTERIOR- Sorority House bathroom

The shower is still running. The bathroom is completely steamed up.

LISA
"Melanie? Melanie, are you still in the shower?"

LISA moves through the steam to

* * *

Damn it. Talby tabbed back to the pages from yesterday. His eyes read through the scripted lines.

"Damn it, damn it, damn it," he grumbled. He reread the line which had airhead Melanie shut off the shower when the lights in the bathroom went out.

"There goes the creepy atmosphere," he mumbled. "All the eerie ambiance of the scene is gone, out the window."

Talby contemplated his next move, stared at the computer screen as if expecting the script to magically fix itself. He was already extremely bored with this project and didn't want to waste any more time or brain cells on it.

Finally, after running his fingers through his hair a couple times and popping his neck, Talby said, "Screw it. Nobody will notice anyway and if they do they'll just write it off that the killer turned the shower back on. The guy's crazy. He's capable of anything." With a condescending smile of satisfaction, he continued his work.

* * *

LISA moves through the steam to the shower stall. She screams when she finds the body of MELANIE on the floor of the stall. MELANIE is wrapped in the bloody shower curtain.

The bathroom door explodes open.

From the POV of THE SLAYER, the camera rushes in towards LISA. LISA screams, reacts by kicking THE SLAYER in the groin. THE SLAYER doubles over, drops his hunting knife.

Quickly, LISA grabs for the hunting knife. With one quick jab, she stabs THE SLAYER in the chest. THE SLAYER tumbles backwards out of the bathroom and collapses onto the floor in the hallway. His body is still.

LISA stands in the bathroom for a long moment sobbing, staring out at THE SLAYER.

From the POV of LISA, we see THE SLAYER lying in the hall. His chest is not moving. Blood is pouring from the knife wound.

LISA drops the hunting knife. She moves out to the hall, stands over the body of THE SLAYER. Finally, she reaches down and pulls free the mask coving THE SLAYER'S FACE.

LISA
"Oh, my God. It can't be you. You can't be alive."

* * *

There was a light rapping on his office door. Betty stuck her head in. The woman always reminded Talby of an ostrich.

"Danny wants you in his office in ten minutes. Ms. Cage will be here at ten."

Trying to hold on to his last thought, Talby lost it and looked up from his computer screen irritated.

"What, Betty?"

She could tell he was angry. She said, "Danny wants you in his office for Ms. Cage's reading. He wants you to bring some pages from the script."

"Well, Betty, there won't be any pages of script to bring if I can't finish it."

"I'm sorry." Betty didn't look the least bit remorseful for doing her job as directed by the fat man who signed her paycheck every two weeks.

Calming down, Talby rubbed his eyes and looked up at the receptionist. "I'm sorry, Betty. Danny is driving me crazy with this stupid movie and his bevy of bimbo actresses. Tell him to give me twenty minutes."

"He said ten." With that Betty shut the office door.

Ten minutes, twenty minutes, what did any of it matter, Talby thought. It was all wasted time. Looking back at the computer screen he found his place, trying to regain his train of thought.

* * *

Revealing CHRISTOPHER'S face beneath the mask, the flashback begins, showing CHRISTOPHER as a little boy, living in the sorority house before it was a sorority house with his family. With flash cuts we see CHRISTOPHER'S family killed by a masked killer, one after the other. End flashback sequence with a tight close-up of CHRISTOPHER, wide-eyed and splattered in blood, hiding in a closet.

LISA begins to walk down the stairs, weeping. She stops midway down. CHRISTOPHER'S body is seen on the landing above her.

LISA
"It can't be you."

LISA is still struggling with the revelation that her boy-friend CHRISTOPHER is the killer.

FLASHBACK of LISA finding CHRISTOPHER'S body in the car outside.

Unnoticed, behind LISA, CHRISTOPHER sits up. Hearing the floorboard creak, she turns around and screams.

MARCUS (THE SLAYER)
"I guess my dear dead brother never told you about his identical twin, did he?"

LISA
"No." (She wants to run but she is frozen on the stairs.)

MARCUS (THE SLAYER)
"Oh, yes. Sweet Lisa. Christopher always had everything. He was our parents' favorite. They always doted on the little bastard. That's why I killed them."

Go to FLASHBACK of young MARCUS standing over the murdered bodies of his parents. CHRISTOPHER is cowering in the closet.

MARCUS (THE SLAYER)
"I watched you tonight, Lisa. You think you're so goddamn beautiful, so goddamn special." (Smiling, MARCUS begins to slowly walk down the stairs towards her.) "I took you tonight, when you thought I was Christopher. I tasted you."

LISA lashes out toward MARCUS. They struggle on the stairwell until MARCUS pushes LISA away. She tumbles down to the bottom of the steps.

MARCUS (THE SLAYER)
"Now you're going to know what pain really is."

He begins to slowly descend the rest of the stairs.

The front door of the sorority house suddenly bursts open. DETECTIVE SPENCE rushes in with two policemen behind him. They have their revolvers up and ready.

DETECTIVE SPENCE
"Freeze, Marcus!"

MARCUS laughs at the Detective and quickly descends the stairs, racing toward LISA. Before he gets to the bottom step the policemen open fire. MARCUS' body is riddled with gunshots. He falls dead to the floor, next to where LISA sits sobbing.

* * *

"The freaking end," Talby said, saving the final pages of script to its computer file. *It's been a while since I pulled the old Evil Twin reveal*, he thought as the computer took its time saving the input. *I could write the sequel in my sleep.*

When the computer was done saving the file, Talby stood, stretched and then made his way to Danny's office for the morning reading by Annette Cage.

* * *

Ms. Cage and Mr. Slayton were already seated when Talby entered the producer's office.

"Forgive Talby for running late," Danny said with a glance at his scriptwriter. "He was busy putting the finishing touches on the script that is going to make you a star, Ms. Cage."

The blonde girl giggled excitedly.

Talby shook hands then sat in a folding chair on Danny's side of the desk, facing the wide-eyed starlet.

Annette wore a button-down blouse that did little to conceal her breasts and a neatly pressed skirt that showed off enough leg but not too much. She was too smartly dressed to be auditioning for a part in a cheesy stalk-and-slash film. Easily, she could be applying for any kind of office job, a real job.

Herbert Slayton, on the other hand, was dressed in typical young Hollywood. Black shirt, black pants, black shoes, his long black hair was pulled back into a tight ponytail. He seemed slightly withdrawn; Talby figured he was keeping quiet to allow Annette the opportunity to do all the talking since she was the main attraction and not him.

Born in Missouri, Annette Cage left the small town she had grown up in for the glitz and glamour of Hollywood. Her story was no different than most of the young actresses they interviewed. They were surprised to learn that Herbert had been with her from the trip out of her hometown to California. Talby initially figured Herbert had snatched her right off the bus when she arrived in town.

To Danny's delight, Annette Cage had spent plenty of time swinging on the brass poles of various gentlemen's clubs. As far as Danny was concerned, that meant the girl was comfortable with her body around large groups of people and would consent to doing nudity without question if she wanted the job.

"I guess we just need to see what you can do now," Danny said with a big grin. "Did you bring some pages from the new script?" he asked, looking toward Talby.

Before Talby could offer the pages, Herbert Slayton said, "We have our own script." He stood up and moved the chair he had been sitting in out of the way.

"You'll get a great idea of what my third talent is," Annette said with a wink. "I promise." Danny looked like he was going to explode with excitement.

Herbert Slayton took a prop from the shoulder pack he'd brought. The bag had been lying unnoticed at his feet.

Annette Cage situated herself directly in front of Danny's desk and proceeded to enact her prepared scene.

Pretending to read a magazine, Annette reacted to the imagined rings of a nearby telephone. She answered and recited her memorized lines. Herbert stood silently to the side with the prop machete he had taken from the shoulder bag.

Annette talked to nobody for a few minutes, her face reacting in horror to what the make-believe character on the other end of the imaginary phone was telling her.

Talby just shook his head. It was practically a scene from a couple of the teenkill movies he had written for New Hollywood. A mad killer was on the loose. The police say he should be considered extremely dangerous. Lock your doors, bolt your windows…wait a minute, did you hear that?

It took every ounce of energy he had not to get up and leave. The script was finished, a day early even, and all he wanted to do was go home. He deserved a long weekend for the slave conditions of his job. A nice long weekend would be just the thing. It would give him ample time to vegetate and contemplate where his professional career had gone wrong. A bottle of bourbon would help too. But for Danny's sake he kept still, kept quiet. Inside he wanted to scream, pull his hair and run for the door.

As Annette chattered on, Herbert crept slowly behind her. Talby tried not to laugh.

Roughly, Herbert grabbed her from behind, clamping a hand over her mouth. Annette struggled. There was a look of stark terror in her eyes.

Not bad, Talby thought. That was a classic look of horror movie surprise and she had it down.

When the blade came up to her throat, the blonde girl bit down on Herbert Slayton's hand. Cursing, he jerked his hand away, allowing her time enough to scream.

It was not just any scream, but probably the greatest horror movie scream Graham Talby had ever heard. It hit just the right pitch and had just the right treble. It was hard to find actresses who could properly scream and here was one who did it beautifully.

He was convinced there was a part for her in the new movie. Her perfect scream actually revitalized his interest in the project, even if momentarily. When you found someone who could scream like Annette Cage was screaming, you wanted to use her. He wanted to tell her he would hire her if Danny didn't, ask her where she had learned to scream, but Annette Cage didn't stop screaming long enough for him to say anything. Herbert Slayton didn't stop playing his part in the scene either.

The machete blade cut deep into her throat. A gush of crimson poured from the slit, sprayed blood across the room and caught both Talby and Danny completely by surprise.

"Hey," Danny blurted, jumped back in his chair. His desktop was soaked in the wash of red wetness.

Talby wanted them to stop. The blood was a good shock, the retractable machete blade a real surprise, but neither was necessary for the audition. But Talby couldn't stop them. He could hardly think with Annette Cage's shriek whipping around in his skull like a stirred-up nest of angry hornets.

Betty's head popped into the office to make sure everything was okay. A geyser of crimson splashed the ostrich woman, sending her reeling back into the hall choking and coughing on the mouthful of blood.

"Stop it, goddamn it!" Danny was red-faced and yelling but Herbert Slayton did not stop. The young man used the machete blade to saw more vigorously into Annette Cage's supple throat. Her scream was becoming gargled, like she was drowning in her own blood, but Slayton kept the machete blade sawing.

Continuing to struggle, Annette kicked Danny's desk furiously, struggling to get away from the grasp of Herbert Slayton.

When he had severed her throat completely to the bone, Herbert Slayton dropped the bloody machete and grabbed the girl's head with both hands. She continued her gurgled screaming as he twisted her head violently to one side and then to the other. Slayton struggled savagely to snap her head from the spinal cord.

After the booming crack of the shattering bone, everything went silent. Annette Cage finally stopped screaming.

Herbert Slayton stepped back. He was breathing heavily, his face was flushed dangerously red.

The head lolled to one side then to the other. Finally it tumbled off the stump of the girl's neck. Bloody sinews of muscle kept the head from falling but its weight eventually pulled it free. It rolled across the floor, almost as if it knew where it wanted to go, and stopped. The pretty blonde's face, eyes wide open, was staring right up at Talby and the producer.

Talby tasted sour bile bubbling in the back of his throat. He found it impossible to move. Danny was ghost white. He looked like he wasn't breathing. One oversized hand clutched his chest.

Betty lay on the floor in the hallway, completely passed out.

"What did you think?" It was Herbert Slayton. He was smiling. With a white handkerchief he wiped clean the blood from the machete blade.

Strangely, the head on the floor seemed to be smiling too.

Annette Cage had such a pretty smile, even with the specks of blood dotting her white teeth.

Talby thought he was going crazy. Too much time in La-La Land finally rotted his brain to mush. Maybe this was what happened to people when they could no longer cope with the failure that was their career. They went mad.

Surely this was madness.

Her eyes fluttered.

Her nose twitched ever so slightly.

When at last her mouth opened, the only thing that filled the office was that wonderful, perfect scream.

* * *

Talby nearly made it to the bathroom. Collapsing only a couple feet away from the door, he emptied his stomach in the hallway.

Forcing himself to go on, he pushed open the door to his office. Losing his balance, he fell to the floor.

"Oh, God, Jesus, damn." He was mumbling like a lunatic. His entire body was shaking uncontrollably.

"That son-of-a-bitch killed her," he said, conscious of the fact that he was covered in her blood. He smelled it all over him, breathed her into his lungs.

"Christ, no, he killed her. Cut her head right off." Frantically he searched the top drawer of his desk. He found what he was searching. It was a prop handgun he kept in his drawer for when he needed it to act out some of the action scenes he wrote. He had no idea what type of gun it was. It had always served its simple purpose by being there when he needed it. That was all that was ever important.

As long as it scared the psycho, kept him at bay until the cops arrived, it would still be serving its purpose. He made his way on shaky legs back down the hall to Danny's office. Betty was no longer on the floor outside.

Cops, his mind shouted. *Cops! Where were the goddamn cops?* Detective Spence and all the other one dimensional police officers he had ever created always showed up at the most crucial time to save the day in the movies he wrote. Where in the hell where they now?

The only thing Talby could hear was his own heartbeat, which filled his head. It sounded like the frenzied pounding of a trapped man. Cautiously, with the prop handgun extended before him, he entered Danny's office.

Betty was on top of Danny, practically sitting on his great gut, trying to listen for a sign that the fat man was still among the living. Herbert Slayton snapped a smelling salt and rubbed it under Danny's nose, occasionally slapping Danny's cheek with a bloodied hand.

Annette Cage was sitting in the chair she had been murdered in only moments ago. She was rubbing her neck as if suffering pain from a slight kink.

There was no telltale sign that the head on top of Annette Cage's neck had ever been anywhere else. There was not even the slightest scar of where the machete blade severed her throat all the way to her spine.

When she noticed Talby at the door she jumped up with a huge smile and ran over to him. The prop gun fell uselessly to the floor.

"How did I do?" She was beaming, obviously proud of her reading.

Danny stirred awake and screamed when he saw Betty and Slayton in his face.

"Sorry about that," Annette said in a tiny voice, like a kid busted for drawing on the wall with crayons. "I wanted to do good and I guess I got a little too excited. I got messier than I wanted to get."

Talby didn't know how to react. He was at a total loss for words.

This had never before happened in one of scripts. His victims never came back to life.

"So do I get the part or not?"

Feeling winded, like he had just taken a severe punch to his gut, Talby fell back against the wall. He struggled not to lose his balance and fall again.

"I don't know what else I can do to prove I'm perfect for the part. Unless…"

Fear clutched its cold fingers around Graham Talby's heart and he cringed. He didn't know what to expect. Terror froze him where he slumped against the wall.

With a sly grin, Annette Cage began unbuttoning her bloodied blouse.

Lightning Source UK Ltd.
Milton Keynes UK
KOW040045030113

4317UK00001B/15/P

9 781600 763427